In stories that bring to mind Breece D'J Pancake and Harry Crews, but in a voice all their own, Michael Wayne Hampton's characters fight the hard fight—often facing a life and landscape as stubborn and unforgiving as a rusted engine bolt. Told in voices that are remarkable for their authenticity, Hampton's people are memorable, his prose is lapidary in its precision, and his stories are hard to forget.

Rob Roberge, author of *The Cost of Living*

Michael Wayne Hampton is a born storyteller. And that doesn't just mean he can spin a good yarn, the kind that keeps you ear-stuck and tongue-tied, listening hard. He also has the storyteller's art of absolute authenticity, fidelity to hard-knocked voices—while writing prose that lifts and transcends, that fiercely proclaims that through the ugly, all of us are living some kind of beautiful.

Amber Sparks, author of May We Shed These Human Bodies

These are bold, insistent stories of people dancing along the edges of epiphany and oblivion. Hampton's America is ragged, dangerous, and utterly engaging.

Ian Stansel, author of *Everybody's Irish*

Michael Wayne Hampton can inhabit a carnival barker, a beauty queen, a teenaged runaway, or a caregiver at the state mental hospital. In this uncomfortable and unforgettable story collection, he goes deep inside these and other dark and puzzling characters. Misfits perhaps, but we want to get to know them, and sometimes—more often than not—we even fall in love.

Diana Wagman, author of *The Care and Feeding of Exotic Pets*

In *Romance for Delinquents* Michael Wayne Hampton has cut through the sugary version of childhood presented in Hallmark movies to reveal the honest truth: it's a brutal world out there for children…and adults. With gobs of dark humor and insight, Hampton reveals the secret world of boys bent on making mischief at carnivals, of teen girls intent on body piercing at the Salvation Army. The adults in this fine collection are often nothing more than children, at times gullible, at times behaving badly as they try to fulfill society's notions of what adulthood means, from conceiving babies to finding a bride, through whatever means necessary. These fifteen stories—some full-blown stories, some rich vignettes—will have you cringing and laughing, often in the same paragraph, which is a magic trick all by itself.

Marie Manilla, author of *Still Life with Plums*
and *The Patron Saint of Ugly*

Michael Wayne Hampton's stories are compressed interrogations into the pain of trying to live with honor and hurt and the many slight cracks of dignity in a world perhaps better or finer than our own. *Romance for Delinquents* is a love story for recognition and a call for the lost.

Charles Dodd White, author of *Sinners of Sanction County*

Michael Wayne Hampton's *Romance for Delinquents* is as boisterous and bounding with life as any collection you'll read this year…fearless, wickedly funny stories revealing the grotesqueries and heartbreaks of small-town life and love, rendered in pitch-perfect comic prose but with a real tenderness for its stories' oddball, oddly endearing cast of characters underneath. *Romance for Delinquents* is a book to fall in love with.

Joseph Bates, author of *Tomorrowland*

Every sentence in this collection has been worried over in the best way and each story is a tightly written look into the lives of people who are full of despair and hope and everything in between. Hampton has a distinctive voice and these stories sing.

Silas House, author of *The Coal Tattoo*

Like some 'Deadliest Catch' of Middle America, Michael Wayne Hampton ventures into places most inimical to comfort in these stories, casting forth net upon net, and pulling forth creatures of longing, desperation, and stubborn hope--creatures who might very well be us.

                                    Tim Horvath, author of *Understories*

These stories, contemporary as hell, are steeped in the lyric possibility of worlds: a tattoo shop, a carnival, a recognizable Midwestern amusement park, a home for wayward celebrities. The events progress naturally with heartbreaking connections between characters: a jingle writer, the son of a famous scientist, an orderly in a mental hospital, kids in thrift stores, kids in cars, kids in motel rooms. Mike Hampton paints with cultural idioms and reveals wisdom by a turn of phrase.

                              John Minichillo, author of *The Snow Whale*

A rich sadness permeates Michael Wayne Hampton's fine debut collection. "Swimmers" and "The Blessed Event" were two of my favorites, and they also show the author's talent for both long and short forms.

                              Alex Kudera, author of *Fight for Your Long Day*

Hampton can write. Show me anyone who says otherwise and I'll…You know what? I'd prefer not to meet anyone who says otherwise.

                      Joey Goebel, author of *The Anomalies* and *Torture the Artist*

From his faultlessly authentic dialogue to his top-to-bottom portrayal of modern day Appalachia and its people, Michael Hampton's stories resonate with truth and compassion and with just enough foolishness to balance out the ruggedness of their themes. Michael Hampton represents a generation of ridiculously talented young Appalachian writers whose perspectives threaten to revitalize the region's literary identity.

                                  Chris Holbrook, author of *Upheaval*

Foxhead Books

Romance for Delinquents

Michael Wayne Hampton

Foxhead Books

© 2013 by Michael Wayne Hampton. All rights reserved.

No part of this document may be reproduced or transmitted in any form or by any means, electronic, mechanical, photocopying, recording, or otherwise, without prior written permission of the author, with the exception of brief excerpts for inclusion in scholarly works or inclusion in reviews. For permissions or further information, post Potemkin Media Omnibus, Ltd. at 140 E. Broadway Avenue, Tipp City, O. 45371

Hampton, Michael Wayne.

Romance for Delinquents / by Michael Wayne Hampton 206 p. 1.17cm.

1. Fiction. 2. Fiction—Short Stories. I. Romance for Delinquents.

ISBN-13 978-1-940876-02-3

I would like to thank Stephen Marlowe and all the kind folks at Foxhead Books for the opportunity to work with them. Without their belief in me, encouragement, and advice this book wouldn't have been possible.

I'd also like to acknowledge the faculty of Spalding University's MFA program, many of whom guided me through early drafts of the stories contained in this collection.

This book is dedicated to my wife Allison, who tolerated all the long nights I spent locked in my office while I worked on it, and to my mother Mary, who always wanted to be a writer, but passed away before she had the chance.

The stories below originally appeared in the following publications, though most in a different form.

Rabbit Blood : *New Growth: Recent Kentucky Writing*

The Baddest Man in Three Counties : *Fiction Southeast*

Slow Day at the SA : *3AM Magazine*

What They Don't Tell You : *The Southeast Review*

Swimmers : *The Atticus Review*

The Blessed Event : *The Southeast Review*

The Man Who Fell Through the Sky : *Heartlands*

A Long Line of Liars : *Blood Lotus*

Sea Change : *Shaking Like a Mountain*

The Problem with Pretty Girls : *Hoot Review*

Little Animals : *The Rio Grande Review*

Boys and Girls in Motels : *The Pacific Review*

Contents

Rabbit Blood	15
Sock Monkey	29
The Baddest Man in Three Counties	49
Slow Day at the S.A.	51
What They Don't Tell You	65
Swimmers	69
The Blessed Event	97
The Man Who Fell Through the Sky	101
A Long Line of Liars	121
Sea Change	125
The Problem With Pretty Girls	139
The Physics of Love	141
Little Animals	161
Boys and Girls in Motels	181
The Home For Wayward Celebrities	191

Rabbit Blood

My first real love, Darlene, was bound to die in a car wreck. When I was growing up it seemed that was all anybody could talk about. Old men would sit on milk crates with their backs against the ice machine out front of Sailor Brothers' grocery store to watch her fly by. Their gray heads would nod to one another and say, "She's going to catch it one of these days. Yes sir she is."

The worried faces of onlookers would turn in hopes of seeing a county sheriff or state trooper in hot pursuit behind her at last. But no police ever happened to be around to witness her tires screaming against the broken pavement of our little town, and I loved her for it.

Darlene would wheel her Firebird up the blacksnake road that led through the hills past my house towards her own. My daddy said she was going to catch the gravel wrong one time and flip her car over in the creek before anyone could help her. He had seen that kind of thing happen a hundred times since he worked on the volunteer fire department. But that wasn't what happened at all.

What happened to her had more to do with her ex-husband Darrell and her dog, the way she told it. She said it had to do with her daddy and the state of emotion she had been in. But I think it was because she was a rabbit kind of woman. She had too much of that hot rabbit blood in her.

Before Darlene wrecked her Firebird she used to pick me up most mornings during the summer when school was out and take me to her tattoo shop. My daddy must've known where I was going, but he never said anything. I was twelve then and old enough to make my own decisions in his eyes. Besides, he spent most of his time shooting pool or playing Rook down at the fire department.

Her tattoo shop wasn't anything more than a concrete block building with a naked lady painted on the side of it, but it was all she had. She would pick me up because of how good I could draw. My pictures were all over the walls of her shop. "Flash," she called them. When the miners came in to get Woody Woodpecker drilled into their arms or a big Apache chief, what they were pointing at were my masterpieces.

A19 on the wall was a skull I copied off a Slayer T-shirt I saw at

Romance for Delinquents

the county fair. I was spitting up heartbreak over some little girl when I drew it. H11 was a real nice looking motorcycle I drew when I was thinking about how bad I wanted one. Darlene liked all my pictures, but wanted me to learn Chinese writing since it was the big thing. I told her to go to hell, and didn't draw nothing but dragons for a week. No one had any say-so on my work but me. Drawing was something I had always been able to do since I was little. Tooth-marked pencils and Sharpie markers made my mark on the world.

Darlene wasn't kin to me, but it didn't matter. She lived on the same holler so it was all the same. Her daddy, Lucky, raised fighting cocks just up past Zion Baptist Church. He had won enough money fighting them to get her that Firebird. I told my daddy he ought to raise fighting cocks too, but he said he was a rabbit man through and through. Besides, he said, fighting chickens were no good to eat. The way you have to keep their birdbrains wired up on speed takes all the tenderness out of them. Rabbits were different. You could live on rabbit meat. If you got all that hot blood out of them, that is.

My daddy did all right for himself as a rabbit man. Sometimes he would make as much from them little bunnies as he did from his disability checks. I hated helping him with them, but he needed the extra set of hands to move the process along. He explained the truth of the world good and clear. Sometimes you have to let pretty things go just to get by.

When I was younger, I walked out to the cages with him to help with the killing. My daddy would hold them fat papa bunnies up by their ears. Then he would crack their little heads with a crowbar till there wasn't any life left in them. Most of the time it only took one good stroke and they would jerk and go off to their reward without so much as a yelp. After he had cracked one he would toss it on the ground, and it was my job to pass him the next. A big brown rabbit. Whack! A fat white one with dirty fur. Whack! He never saw a tear from me.

The first time I tried to argue with him, saying it was wrong and all since they were helpless, but he told me what he was doing was buying me my Christmas. It was a damn cold truth. My hands went into the cage and I closed my eyes. The trees were turning gold and brown like rotten apples. I thought about getting a dirt bike.

"Here, whack this one Daddy!"

The rabbits were the reason I met Darlene. I would take rabbit meat up to Lucky on Saturdays and he would give me pain medicine in a sandwich bag to take back to my daddy. What he was wasn't a doctor, but someone who knew about pain I guess.

When I met Darlene the first time she was laying out in her backyard on a towel. She had a bikini on that was the color of dandelion fluff with the straps let down. Lucky wasn't home and her man was off on a long haul, so she was out back working on her tan.

"What you got there all wrapped up?" She asked as I made my way through the yard. The chickens started cussing and spitting at me from where they were penned up in the yard. Fighting chickens are like that. It's in their nature.

"Just some rabbit meat for Lucky."

"Well he ain't here and I don't eat it." Her eyes were on the tops of the pine trees scraping against Heaven.

"I'm supposed to bring it for trade. We even went and took all the blood out for him." I looked down at the butcher paper all tied up with string.

"What do you mean you even took the blood out?" She asked over her big white sunglasses.

"You can't eat the rabbit blood." I said.

"Why not?"

"Daddy says rabbit blood is too hot. It puts run into you."

"So," she said.

"It'll make you run too fast for your own good."

I smiled down at where her bikini straps hung loose under her arms. She was the first real girl I had seen that way. By then, she was almost out of high school.

She could have slapped me straight across the face or kissed me right there, but in the end she just wrapped the towel around herself and went inside. I waited in the yard while she got daddy's medicine for trade. Something inside of me made me shake like I was pissing on an electric fence.

"Here you go," she said. "Now don't you sneak around here no more."

"I won't come back again if you don't want me to," I said. The way she stood with her hands on her hips made her look like the girls

I had seen on the calendar at the firehouse.

"I didn't say to stay away," she smiled the way girls did in the back of the school bus, "just don't be sneaking."

From then on out, Darlene and I were good friends.

Every day I would go up her house and she would teach me about all kinds of stuff. We would practice kissing one day, then the next she would tell me about how to make a chicken real mean so when it gets in the ring you'll know it's a winner. She told me how love is just an excuse for people to stop living. I told her how drawing a perfect circle is about the hardest thing anyone can do.

She had herself a lot of sweethearts on the side by then. I wasn't interested in that though, since I was still young and kissing was all I could handle. Back then kissing was better than Christmas and dirt bikes put together. I would ride home from the tattoo shop with her in Lucky's truck, its tires kicking up gravel and pine needles, grinning like my daddy with a bellyful of medicine.

It was when Darlene got that Firebird that things started to change. She had quit school by then, since she owned her own business and they couldn't teach her nothing anyhow. She would pick me up to go draw for her, but we didn't talk much.

Her man Darrell had been asking questions about other men and where his checks had been going, she said. He had been talking to a lawyer in town too. It broke her heart. She would just smoke those big long cigarettes the whole way to the tattoo shop without so much as a glance my way. One minute she would say her man was the worst son of a bitch she had ever seen. The next she would talk like he was the hero of us all. Love does that to girls.

Once we got to the shop, she would go off to get her hair done or talk to her pastor. She had papers to sign and a hell of a custody battle brewing over their little beagle dog. I started to do the tattooing for her when I had the chance.

The majority of the customers would shy away when they saw it was only me there with the gun, but not all. If the men were half-lit and hollering when they walked in, every once in awhile I could convince them that I was the man for the job seeing as I had drawn all the pictures hanging up in the shop. I always did my best work on the wild ones who let me drill into them: Jesus on the cross, eagles flying through the sky, dog's showing their teeth. None of them ever complained. I would sop the blood off them with a dish rag while they praised my needlework. Then I would stuff their money in a Mason jar Darlene kept under the table and hope she would be impressed. Most of the time though, she would just tussle my hair and take me home without so much as a thank you.

Darlene let me practice tattooing on watermelons and cantaloupes out back of her shop when there wasn't any picture drawing to do. She said that was the best way to learn to use the tattoo gun since the melons had pores like people do. The only thing was that you couldn't practice stretching the skin on them, which was real important. She told me I would never be a real tattoo artist until I learned to stretch the skin no matter how many drunks I needled on. I didn't care what she said. All she did was trace down what I put on the walls anyway.

With summer ending, I worked real hard on getting my drawing down right. The tattooing was going slow since less and less people wanted a kid near them with Darlene's jerry-rigged tattoo gun and she was hardly ever there. I started thinking about running away from home. Maybe getting an art scholarship to one of those schools I had seen on the television commercials. I was sure I had enough practice with all the wall drawing and needling I had done, so I sent away for an art test. It was for a real art school in Chicago. I had seen its commercial in between Gilligan's Island reruns when I killed time at my Mamaw's. It made perfect sense.

Darlene got back to tattooing when the courts slowed things down. That gave me time to sit out back by the rotten cantaloupes, all scarred up with tigers and devils, and practice for my art test. I was torn between drawing the turtle or the pirate. For awhile I just practiced drawing a perfect circle on some old grocery bags. But then I decided on the pirate and spent all day getting his earring and hat to look the way it did on the pamphlet the art school sent me.

I folded my test up real careful and gave it to Darlene to mail for me. It was going all the way to Chicago, but she said I had a good chance. I agreed with her. I'd had extra practice drawing on the inside of the songbooks in church.

Darlene's man Darrell had taken off trucking long enough to settle things with her once and for all, but he never seemed to make much headway. One night I would see him in her car when she drove by my house, the radio would be blaring and their arms would be gliding out the windows in the breeze, then the next day I would hear her yelling into the phone about how terrible a man he was. He would yell so loud back at her from wherever he was that his voice would come through the receiver and bounce off the walls of the shop. He would name men I had never heard of, call her every bad word he could sputter out, but he would never hang up. He would just go on being hateful till she would tear up and slam down the phone. Love does that to men.

The last day of summer, my daddy sat on the porch brushing out the fur he had pulled off some bunny after the fact. He watched me walk up from where Darlene dropped me off at the bridge and shook his head.

"Son come over here," he said as he wiped his hands clean on his pants legs. He had one of them rabbit's shirts dangling in his hands, bleeding in the wind.

That was when he told me about Lucky's troubles and that I couldn't see him or Darlene anymore. He told me to act like I never even heard tell of them. The sheriff had helicopters in the air. Undercover agents had been getting medicine from Lucky. My daddy had heard all about it at the firehouse.

The next morning cruisers from the county and the state filled up the parking lot of Zion Baptist Church. Reporters had driven in from Hazard for the Mountain News. All I could hear were sirens and the sound of those fighting cocks tearing at their cages to get at the police. By the time it was dark outside, everything was still as Sunday morning again. Out barefoot in the yard, I was spitting up heartbreak all over again.

Staying away from Darlene was something I couldn't do. I still had all my good drawings up at her shop. I wanted to know if she had heard back about my art test. I wanted to make sure she was all right. That was the way I loved her.

It took a while for me to figure out which school bus went by her shop, and when I did I went to see her. It meant walking home and catching hell, but it was worth it.

That morning I snuck some rabbit meat out of the freezer for Lucky. I figured he would be missing it when they sent him away. It thawed out in my backpack by the time the school bus got to her shop, but I figured he'd find a way to eat it. The meat looked like those bags you see up on poles in hospital shows.

When I got to the shop it was unlocked and empty. All my pictures were gone, and the only thing left was her tattoo rig lying by the trash can with the battery missing. There was nothing there for me. I dropped the meat by the door of the shop and started down the road feeling like a fool.

At home, the porch lights where burning bright. Lightning bugs kicked along the rows of corn. My daddy sat on the porch waiting for me, but went inside once he saw me cross the bridge. He knew where I stood and there was no use talking about it. Besides, without his medicine he was in no shape for fighting. Since Lucky had been taken away, he spent most of his time on the porch staring down the road, as if he thought Lucky might drive past at anytime. Sometimes he would stay up all night miserable and hoping.

Under the covers that night, I prayed for Darlene and the Art Institute of Chicago.

Beagles howled off sad in the dark. My daddy's emergency pager from the firehouse started to beep so loud it made me have to pull the pillow over my head just to get some peace. I already knew what had happened.

Sunday morning I walked to church alone. My daddy had been up all night and didn't want to talk about it. He always spared me the stories about picking up heads off the highway or fishing somebody's kid out of a silt pond. No matter how bad I begged to know who got killed, he saved that for the Lord and the newspaper.

I walked to church, and as soon as I got within eye-shot of the doors Darlene's man Darrell took me by the arm. We were on the road before he said word one to me.

"We ain't together," Darrell said. "It was my damn dog in the first place. I told her. She should have stayed in school. I told her."

He was talking to the steering wheel as much as to me, rolling his window up and down for no reason at all.

When we made it to the hospital he told me what room she was in. He wasn't about to see her for fear he'd kill her. That was why he brought me he said. I walked in the closest thing to kin she had left.

In the room they had her hooked up to all kinds of machines. She was covered with stickers. Her nose was raw and red. Her eyes looked like someone had just snuck up on her. The rest of her was all different colors of blue and green.

When she could, she told me about taking too much medicine for her pain and all, about wanting to steal her dog back from Darrell, about what they were charging Lucky with and losing control of her Firebird at the tree line. None of it made any sense.

"Why'd you run all the way out there to steal back a damn dog?" I wanted to say the things her daddy would have if he could have been there, but I was too hot at her.

"I don't know," she said. "It just came over me last night. I got all hateful at the world."

She told me she threw away my art test. She told me I was just a dumb kid. She told me about losing her tattoo shop to the bank. She told me to leave her be.

"Did you find the rabbit meat I left for your daddy at least?" I asked.

"I tried some from the freezer to see what the fuss was about," she said. "What you brought was dropped off yesterday was ruined. The flies were buzzing it out front of the shop. Don't you have any sense? You know Daddy's locked up."

Her eyes started to move away as sleep came over her. I pulled her arms over her chest like the angels in the church. I fished the marker I had brought for the songbooks out of my pocket and started to draw on her while she slept. I stretched her skin tight like a real artist and drew a chicken like her daddy had on her face, standing strong and nasty against the sun. I put a little heart on that chicken with my initials in it. The sun behind it was as close to a perfect circle as I'd ever come.

After seeing her in that bed I never passed another bunny to my daddy, dirt bike or no dirt bike. There are things you can't explain. Mysteries like perfect loves and people born with hot rabbit blood in their veins. Damn cold truths.

Sock Monkey

The little monsters were already sweating themselves silly under their rubber masks, but the promise of a twenty dollar bill for one night's work was worth fighting back their bellies until the car stopped. Jack was almost twelve, and had to hold his breath to keep out the paint smell from the Frankenstein head he wore. Randy was ten, and inside his Wolfman mask he imagined all the girls he'd scare to death. Up in the front of the car, Sherri just wished the damned radio worked.

"I don't know why you had to bring those knotheads with us. You know they'll end up getting lost," David said as if she was paying attention to him. He had come to understand that being closer to her mother's age meant that only about half of anything he said ever reached her, and was sure that nothing her mother said ever did. If he was a different man he would have kept on loving her mother, instead of paying favors like this to make up for tearing her up when they were young.

"They're my brothers, David," Sherri said as she patted her forehead dry with a paper napkin. "Besides, they're working tonight."

"It may be Halloween, but no carnival should hire young'uns. Especially two like them." David threw his toothpick out the window before sticking another one in his craw. He'd worked at the county jail long enough to know what happened to juvenile delinquents with a little money. "If it was me I'd lock them in the barn, give them each a broom handle, and see which one came out the winner."

"Shut up and drive," Sherri said as she straightened her starched cheerleading skirt. "We're going to have a big time tonight."

The Oriental Carnival had rolled into town at the first of the week. Trailers loaded down with the bones of tents and rides had pulled off the interstate followed by vans packed with stuffed bears, green ring toss bottles, and cages filled with creatures from the other side of the world. The promise of adventure was thick in the air.

Down at the flattest spot in town, a makeshift airstrip used by the coal company's planes, the rides and game shacks were assembled under flood lights which illuminated the shadows of thin men moving steel poles and clapboard signs. It was nearly Halloween and a chill had settled in the air. The carnival was there to make what it

Romance for Delinquents

could before heading back to Florida where they would park it until summer. Under the lights rough men prayed for a hard frost to come soon so that they could turn back home, and forget all that they had done.

The whole town waited to see the menagerie and a good number of them had been recruited to make sure things ran smoothly. Sherri and the rest of the cheerleaders from the high school were there to dance for the crowd after the string band finished. Her brothers were in charge of picking up trash when there wasn't a need to scare the people getting their tickets torn. When you live in the mountains any change in scenery is appreciated, and there was talk that some of the carnival's men had been as far as California. This made them all handsome and debonair regardless of how wiry and wild they appeared.

David was at the carnival under both protest and duty. Everyone at the jail had been volunteered to help with crowd control, and even a couple of the locked up boys who were behind on their child support were given a weekend pass so that they could work and make up a little restitution. As he parked his car in the overgrown grass he already expected trouble, half-hoped for it, and wished the Sheriff had at least given him a gun. After all, they went fishing together and he could shoot better staggered then most of police force could right out of the church house.

"Now you remember what I told you," David said. "You do

your twirls and eat your cotton candy, but by ten o'clock you better be back at this car. Your mom will kill me if you end up stolen away by some hack who guesses people's weight for a living."

Sherri pulled her ponytail tight and traced her lipstick lines clean with a pinky finger. "I'll be here. Just don't get yourself eaten by no lion." By the time they'd agreed that neither of them would get killed or kidnapped the monsters were gone.

"Damn it!" David tucked his shirttails into his jeans and scanned the field. Two rubber heads bobbled back on bodies running toward the crowd. "Do they know where to be?"

"They know," Sherri said. "Major Bill gave them a paper for Mommy to sign."

"Major Bill. How come every carny has to play like he was in the Army?"

"It's showbiz. Now I have to places to be! Go arrest somebody for peeing outside." Pompoms in hand, Sherri walked straight toward the throng of miners and pudgy children. David regretted ever promising her mother he'd look after her kids. If he hadn't almost married her in high school he would have never sworn to see after them, but given the fact that she was out of work and looking after her mother it seemed the least he could do. When he was alone he often wondered if her life would have been roses if he hadn't lost his nerve.

Once he made his way through the crowd, the Sheriff had him and the rest of the crew circle up so he could give them the rundown for the night. While most of the men were left to wander around and keep an eye out for trouble, so long as they didn't start tossing balls or talking to some woman, David was given a flashlight and put in charge of the parking. He tried to argue, knowing how hard it would be for him to watch the kids if he was waving cars in and out, but the Sheriff was up for re-election in a month and not about to have any of his decisions questioned for fear of seeming weak. After all, there was no guarantee that he'd had enough fish fries to secure his position. Flashlight in hand, David walked the two hundred yards back to the road to get his bearings.

By the time the evening was picking up heat Sherri stood at attention by the bandstand and listened to Amber threaten the junior varsity girls about making them all look bad. As senior cheer captain Amber was in charge since the squad's sponsor was still recovering from another elective surgery. It would be her ass if things didn't go right.

"You act like ladies tonight," Amber said flatly as she pushed her shoulders back. "We are here as representatives of our school and America. These people came to see us so do it right. Don't give the preacher any sermons."

The girls nodded and checked their watches. Sherri had an hour before she was set to dance and was glad that both her brothers and David were nowhere in sight. At least that way she figured she could have a little fun.

"Listen for the music ladies," Amber said raising a hand to her ear. "At eight o'clock the band will start up The Star-Spangled Banner, and I better see you all standing right by me."

The girls giggled and scattered out in a dozen different directions. In less than a minute there wasn't a hair bow in sight.

Jack saw the padlock first. Through his rubber eyeholes he scoped it shining heavy where it hung on the chain. If all the other trucks hadn't had their doors splayed wide open he wouldn't have given it a second thought, but since Major Bill had seen fit to lock away whatever treasure it held inside from the rest of the world he couldn't help but wonder what magic might be stowed away inside. At any rate, if things went bad he figured twenty dollars would pay for a lock. It didn't take him long to find Randy. His brother was crouched down with his hands on knees and his Wolfman pulled back. "I can't breathe in that thing!" He said before spitting plastic hairs out of his mouth. "It ain't worth no twenty dollars if I can't breathe."

"Forget that dummy head and come on," Jack said. "We need to find us a crowbar."

It seemed that tools were in short supply as the boys searched the grounds for a pry bar. They crawled under the big rigs and found a tire jack, but didn't figure it would do them much good. It wasn't until Randy shimmied underneath the bandstand's skirt and came up with a steel pipe left unattached that they felt there was any promise of breaking in. Randy walked through the crowd like he had somewhere important to be before hiding the pipe in a patch of tall weeds on the bank by the truck. Then the two split up and agreed that they'd wait till everybody was watching the girls cheer about being American before making their move. Night was coming on.

David's arm felt like it was about to twist out of his shirt sleeve when Ronnie Murphy rolled up to him in his rusty Jeep Cherokee. His boy Arthur was painted up like a vampire with a talcum powder white face and fake ketchup blood dribbles on his cheeks.

"You want a beer?" Ronnie asked with one arm motioning back toward his cooler. Ronnie knew that his buddy was trying to live Christian, but since he had past success in inspiring honest backsliding he figured it was worth a shot. Besides, he hated the idea of drinking alone in the field until his boy finished whatever he was sent there to do.

"Can't drink here. You know them people will report me. I got to wave cars back and forth until this mess is over," David said eyeing the cooler in the back. "What's he supposed to do anyway?"

"I don't know. Run around like a ghost or something." Ronnie lit a cigarette and listened to the cars behind him honk hate his way. "Come on man. I got a jar back there too."

"How much they paying him?"

"Twenty. That's what the paper he brought home said at least."

"I'll give him thirty to wave cars with this flashlight. I can't stand no more of this."

Arthur slid out of the jeep and David fished two bills from his wallet before taking his place. "Waste of my time anyway." Then they were off.

Sherri had a fold of dollar bills from her mommy tucked into her sports bra, and with precious little time to kill she figured she had better spend it quick. She tried her luck at the ring toss game, but found even her best throws weren't good enough to land a ring on one of the fat-necked bottles. She fared better when it came to throwing darts at water balloons, and walked away with a stuffed sock monkey after seven tries. With her funds running low it occurred to her that she better ride what she could before her time came to perform. That's when she made her way toward The Scrambler.

Lined up behind tense mothers and kids juiced on too much candy and Mountain Dew, she feared that she wouldn't be able to take a turn before the music signaled her to shout out and pump her fist in the air with the rest of the squad. Two dozen people took baby steps while the aluminum contraption spun folks tied into their seats around under disco lights. Whitesnake and Motley Crüe screamed hard rock from speakers mounted on poles. It seemed any chance for fun had been stolen away from her until a slick boy walked up to make time.

"You wanna ride this," He said all white-toothed smile. "I can get you a VIP pass." His arms were crossed with scars, but his eyes watered soft as a hound dog.

"What makes me so special," Sherri asked with her arms crossed. "I ain't no VIP."

"You're wrong," the boy said as he set a hard grin on her. "Pretty girls like you are always VIPs." He laced his arm into the crook of hers, delighting in how soft and warm it was, and led her to the front of the line. "Here in a minute I'm going to show you a real ride. We're going to have us some fun."

Jack listened to the band tear through "Fox on the Run" and "Kiss Me Quick and Go" while Randy stomped a rain dance in a circle of dust with his Wolfman head gyrating from where he'd pushed it back on his crown. The banjos and guitars beat a fire into the boys until they had half-forgot their plan. It wasn't until the caller got on the microphone to slow down the evening that the two remembered their plot. The crowd inched closer toward the bandstand while the musicians in matching white hats played a song about some woman wandering the hills in a veil. There was no need to wait for the cheering.

"Here's how it's going to go," Jack said as he beat the pipe against the palm of his bony hand. "I'm going to wedge this pipe in there and jump up against that door. Then you're going to grab a hold of me and yank with all you got."

Randy pulled his head back on and roared while his dirty fingers clawed the air.

"I reckon it will take the both of us."

With the pipe wedged behind the lock, Jack jumped up and kicked his legs stiff. Randy looped both arms around his brother and jerked with all the muscle he could muster. Just when Jack felt like he was going to break a rib if his little brother squeezed him any harder something popped in the door and the two fell back to solid ground. The rig door opened a foot from where the chain sagged down, but the lock held tight to mock them.

"I could get every last one of them," David said louder than he meant to as he looked through the scope of Ronnie's deer rifle at children chasing one another between wrapped up teenage lovers. As he stared through the crosshairs he could make out the faces of everyone he had ever known. The whole town was down range and ready.

"Be careful now," Ronnie said as he opened another beer to chase down the moonshine he'd gotten in trade from the county coroner. "I can't remember if the damn thing is loaded or not."

David took a swig from the jar before lifting the butt of Ronnie's rifle back up to his shoulder. "You know buddy, there's a lot of people across that field I'd love to take a shot at if I had it in me."

"You ain't got the guts to shoot nobody, and we have a half a cooler left."

"What time is it?"

"Not over yet. All I know." Ronnie rolled off the hood to stretch the kinks out of his back. "I just wished I hadn't let his mommy talk me in to bringing him. What's the good in bringing your kid to the carnival if they can't have no fun. He can't keep his mind to nothing no how."

David swept the scope back over to the road where half the cars snaked their way through a barricade to park closer to the rides. Arthur had spirited himself away and taken the county's flashlight with him. For a minute he considered shooting the tires out of the cars, but better judgment prevailed when the prospect of getting fired hit him.

"Shit."

Sonny was his name. He offered it while strapping Sherri into the Scrambler. The nylon belts bit into her shoulders and crushed the sock monkey against her heart.

"You got great legs girl," Sonny said. "You ready for your ride?"

Sherri set her jaw. "Sure I am. You don't scare me none."

"Not yet I don't," Sonny said, the softness leaving his eyes. "Not yet." Then he made his way across the inverted sheet metal plane to secure all the other joy seekers in place.

Sherri closed her eyes and listened to the sound of footfalls on metal, of belts snapping into place against the rumble of the music and crowd. Her ears searched for the sad wail of the caller or the anxious heartbeat of the stand-up bass plowing through the night air, but found only quiet in the distance. Her time was running out.

Jack ran hard to catch Randy, but with the scare still bolting through him there was little chance that he could get a hold of him. He stopped when his air left him and watched the mangy brown head of his brother dart left by the water pistol booth. The only hope left was that Randy had the good sense to keep his mouth shut about what had slid out of that trailer.

Frankenstein head in hand, Jack worked stories through his brain. He could claim that him and Randy were at the dunk tank the whole time and would soak his shirt to prove it if he could reach his brother in time to gain agreement on the lie. If he couldn't find him, he would have to blame it on him since he had no intentions of taking any heat himself. He only wished that his mommy hadn't found the BB gun he'd tucked down his pants before David picked them all up. If she had let him keep it, he reckoned he could have shot that monster before anyone saw it and lifted it back inside. Alone in the noise of the crowd, he prayed it didn't eat someone's kid or puppy dog before the cops found it.

The straight lines of cars creeping in and out that David had left were a tangled mess by the time he walked himself back to the road. A pickup truck had rear-ended a Grand Am that had tried to cut left through the barriers along the entrance. Both drivers had stopped and were ready to kill one another. He waited for awhile, hoping they'd all calm down and figure it out for themselves, but when it was clear that they were more set on beating each other's brain in he had no choice but to move in. He fished his badge out of his shirt pocket and started waving it in the air. For a minute no one gave him much mind until they realized he was shaking a rifle in the other hand. That helped them see the light.

What struck Sherri most were the colors. The flood lamps and Christmas lights streaked lines of green and red against the night sky where the stars were shining. Golden traces entered the stream above until only rainbow bands and half-formed faces shouting laughter melted into the black space before her. She tried her best to push her back into the seat and keep her eyes open to prove she was strong. Her guts tied themselves in knots as she spun, and in a brief pass she heard the national anthem elbowing itself in between power chords. There was no escape in sight.

"Stop it!" She cried until she about lost her voice. "Stop!"

Sherri's fingers yanked at the belt, but could find no release. Blood rushed up to her neck and she feared if Sonny didn't stop it soon she was going to go black. Sonny perched an arm up on the controls and nodded her way grinning. The whole time he kept belly laughing as if he'd heard the funniest thing in the world.

"Stop! Let me go!"

Jack had Randy on his belly and was working his legs into a figure four when he saw the city police go running through the crowd. When he let go of his brother's ankle he caught a good kick to the chin, which led to another attempt to pin reason into him. "They saw it!" Jack squealed before dropping an elbow onto him. "Let's go watch them try and catch it."

Randy pulled his mask back down over his head and the two were off.

David felt like he had a woodpecker stuck between his eyes, but he was able to pull himself together enough to fashion what was left of the barricades back in place so that the cars moved like they should. The liquor and beer were winning the war inside him by that time, so he decided to go find the kids and get out of there before anyone important got a good whiff of him.

He wasn't getting any overtime for his efforts and Sherri's mommy would to be off work soon. The noise around him was doing its best to kill the only good buzz he'd had in weeks.

David propped the rifle on his shoulder and made his way toward the games. That's when the Sheriff caught him by the neck and flung him into a run. There was no time to argue.

When the national anthem ended and the cheers came on, Sherri began to pray. She apologized to Jesus for being a gossip and kissing a boy behind the church during vacation Bible school. While the world wheeled she called for grace to wash away all her sins and put her feet back on solid ground, but the more she bit her lip in a session of desperate repentance the faster she was tossed around. The two kids next to her were red-faced from bawling. The other people on the ride clung on for life and screamed. Sonny lit a smoke and eyed her as he put his hands together in prayer. He had her. The lights began to dim.

Back behind the trailers, where the field sloped down into a drainage ditch, a line of county deputies and part-time city policemen shined their flashlights onto thirty feet of meanness moving through the water below.

"What do you think it is?" David asked.

"Snake," one of the deputies said, "a big one."

"I know that, but what kind?"

"Who the hell cares," the Sheriff said. "One of you has to catch it."

"I ain't touching it," one of the deputies said. "You know them things eat pigs."

"That thing can't eat a pig," the Sheriff said. "They eat dogs and rats."

"Then I sure ain't going in," David said. "Dogs are a lot meaner than pigs."

The Sheriff chewed on that for a second and decided losing a man to a snake was bad politics. "One of you go and find that Major Bill. It's his property and his problem."

Stooped behind the line of men, Jack and Randy agreed that it was best if they found him first. That way the story of how it got out would be theirs to tell. They walked away from the circle of lawmen and discussed which one of them it would be best to pin it on. David was the prime on their list.

The boys found Major Bill counting dollar bills into a tackle box out front of the main tent. Through the flap they could see a big-bellied man sticking a lit torch down his throat while worried parents covered the eyes of their wiggling children. "We ain't seen nothing all night," Randy moaned. "Working is for suckers."

"We'll figure that out later now," Jack said as he slid an arm over his brother. "Right now we have to save our skin." He walked solemnly up to Major Bill and offered the sad tale of how his mommy's friend had gotten drunk and tried to pry open a trailer. With his eyes pointed down on the Major's alligator boots he said the whole county sheriff's department was about to kill the monster snake one of their own set loose if he didn't stop them, and that he was about to cry at the thought of it catching a bullet. The whole time he'd been working on a stream of tears to cement his grief, but there was no need for it. The Major was already hot-footing off to save his baby, bowie knife at the ready in case one of the rubes tried to claim jurisdiction.

"What now," Randy asked, as he stuffed wads of cash into his pants.

"Now nothing," Jack answered. "Let's go watch that fat man catch himself on fire."

David found the pardon to slip away from the crowd when the Major came up on the men fuming and waving his knife. The Sheriff drew down on the Major, but didn't dare to shoot him since a boy from the paper had come up on the scene with his camera out. A Burmese python would be news enough without attaching it to a murder. When calmer heads prevailed the Major passed his boots off to one of the city boys and waded down into the dark to drag his darling back home. The reporter from the paper took pictures of the conflict while flashlights brightened the field of battle. The deputies put their hands on their knees and made their bets in between whoops of "Get em! Get 'em!" There was no way of telling which one they cheered for.

David had taken more than his share from Ronnie's cooler, and the carnival was a bad place to be out of his head. Every two steps somebody bumped him sideways, ran in front of his feet, or nearly shouldered him to the ground. The strobe lights left him squinting to piece the landscape together. Everywhere he turned music blared from the shacks broken only by squeals of delights and indecipherable yelps. For a minute he stood still and let the instincts he'd honed through years of hell-raising come to the forefront. He lifted his head tall, stuck his badge out in one hand, and poked the rifle in front of him like a soldier. Then he paced his way back toward the bandstand concentrating on each step. He was determined to find the kids, and either shoot them all or pack them home. It didn't matter which.

    Jack and Randy followed the herd of people rushing to get out of the tent to see the snake wrestling. Word had spread fast, and rumor had it that a good third of Major Bill's forearm had already disappeared down the gullet of his darling. Masks in hand they wormed their way through air thick with popcorn smoke until the barrel of a rifle impeded their progress.

    "Take off those dummy heads and get right," David said as he pushed the boys into a line. "We got to find your sister and get out of here before we all catch Hell. Ain't nothing positive can happen now." He propped the rifle over his shoulder and marched the two back toward the bandstand determined to find Sherri so that he could spirit the heathens back to their mother before his legs left him. Before he could a thunder of panic filled the air and stirred what little sense of duty he had left in him to go investigate.

    Sparks kicked up from underneath The Scrambler as it wheeled faster than a Maytag set on high dry. A half circle of people waved fists and threw pop cans up at the scaffolding by the contraption where Sonny danced, waved his shirt in the air, and whistled down at the crowd. "Come on!" He sneered. "Let me hear it!" There was only madness in the carnival dark, and the sound of lungs giving out as they swooped by. "What you going to do now!"

David took off his belt and roped the boys together at the ankle. "If you all run off I'll shoot you both dead." The boys stood quiet and nodded, each regretting missing that snake choke down Major Bill. After David made his way to the back of the scaffold they began searching the ground for good rocks to throw at him.

"One hand pulls me up and then I step," David talked his way through it. Climbing with a rifle was a sure way to blow his head off, but he figured he was the only authority left to stop the machine. Even a maniac had to understand a gun in his face. Sonny kept one hand on the controls and spit tobacco juice down at the crowd and cheered them on. These people came for a scene, he thought, and now boy they got them one. It wasn't until the rifle stabbed the square of his back to where he almost fell boot heels over crew cut that he lost his sense of humor.

"Which one of these buttons stops it?" David asked, fighting to keep an eye open.

"The big red one," Sonny said as he pulled his shirt back on. "You people don't know how to have any fun."

David held the stock of the rifle tight against his shoulder as he punched the stop button with his free hand. The circling steel creaked down revolution by revolution while rocks and pop cans shot up through the sky at him and his prisoner.

"It's over!" David shouted down to where the crowd fussed. "I got him."

"Yeah boss," Sonny said with his hands braced on the railing. "You sure got me good."

It took Sherri a good while to stop crying once they all got back in the car and pulled away. David wished he could comfort her, but his head felt like it was full of nails. All he wanted was a cold glass of water and some sleep. Finally, in the silence that came after they made it through town, he offered her what tenderness he could find.

"How'd your cheering go honey?" He could feel a change in her, as if something was missing.

"I didn't make it," Sherri said almost too quiet for him to hear. "I told him to stop. I did. I kept yelling for him to stop."

"You got to learn that boys don't always stop when you tell them to, especially boys like that one. You remember that now."

Sherri sat in the passenger seat turning herself over inside. Behind her, Randy counted his loot while Jack worked on tearing her sock monkey limb from limb.

The Baddest Man in Three Counties

Israel Spurlock came out of his mama filled with the devil. She thought giving him a Bible name would help calm him, but it didn't save him from a life of hatefulness. He knocked out teeth from Leslie County to Pikeville before he got kicked off the football team. It wasn't worth driving a thug around who couldn't make it half a quarter without getting a flag.

Once, when I was in middle school, he snuck into a DARE assembly and kicked the shit out of Randy White for talking to his girlfriend. It took two teachers and a librarian to pull him off of that boy. His girlfriend Jamie was thirteen then. He must have been seventeen at least, because by the time I moved up to high school he'd been dropped out for at least a year. I heard the stories though.

My brother told me that he got into it with Israel during the ASVAB test, and still couldn't hear out of his left ear. He said that Israel had a knife with him, but didn't dare pull it in front of those bald-headed Marines.

Darrell Wayne told me that Israel used to come up to the slow kids on the bus, and beat them while hollering "Ring the bell motherfucker! Ring the bell!"

The kids would ball up in the isle with their coats pulled over their heads and shout, "Ding! Ding! Ding!" Then he'd stop. Pull his hat down. That was his joke.

After he disappeared all the stories I heard were crazy. A girl told me he'd moved to Louisville, joined a gang, and was nearly burned to death when some other boys with gas cans caught him sleeping on a couch. Others said he'd found Jesus, and moved away to build houses in Mexico. I'd like to believe that—all church kids hope for redemption—but I can't.

What I picture is that Israel moved to Lexington like the rest of us. No jobs here unless you want to work at the prison or the school. You see the same people eventually. I imagine he has two kids by now, and a wife that can't stand him but can't leave him out of fear and need. In my mind they all live in a little house with rusty tricycles out front, and inside, all the walls have holes.

Slow Day at the S.A.

At first the two girls had considered using a paperclip they found while rummaging underneath the cash register's drawer, but when they straightened it out it didn't look sharp enough to work. Its point was flat, and there was the fear that it might suddenly bend at an awkward angle when they tried to push it through. Next they thought that a thumb tack they pulled from a cork board in back might do the job, but it was only a stubby point far too short for the task at hand. Later in the morning they debated using a ten-penny nail they had foraged from a tool kit neither of them could remember seeing before, but decided that the hole it would leave might take days to close if it ever did. Finally, Kayla found a long hat pin stuck in the lapel of a stiff cotton nurse's uniform and both girls decided it was the best they could do.

"This will work," Kayla said, as she held the end of the hat pin to the flame of her cigarette lighter to sterilize it.

They knew it was important to use something sharp. The night before, Rachel's brother Tommy had told them a story about a kid he knew named Jackson. The girls had mentioned their project to him to seem grown up after his stories of college hazing died down. He had told it like a campfire story, which gave the girls the impression that he was trying to scare them. For his part Tommy had considered it a warning, and shared the story with them in the hope that it would take the thrill out of their plan.

Tommy described Jackson as a real emo wreck, the kind of kid who wore black all the time and worked hard to look like he was always on the brink of tears. The two had met at a summer camp at the local state university for gifted and talented high school students. For the first month Jackson never said a word to anyone, and spent most of his time alone in their bare dorm room mulling over French poetry. He was working on a paper about Rilke or some other mopey poet for college credit.

Halfway through their program Jackson had become obsessed with "new tribalism," and Tommy was sure it was because of a girl. He stretched out his ear lobes until they held obsidian rings the size of quarters. He branded his arms with a lighter and coat hanger for personal research to include in the essays he was writing about scarification. The program heads wanted to send him home, but somehow he got a paper accepted to a conference in the city so they turned the other cheek and began to encourage him. Tommy stopped talking at that point to lend room for a dramatic pause.

After Jackson had lifted welts on his arms and stretched out his ears to the point of needing cosmetic surgery, Tommy explained, he got into piercing. He put a bone through the septum of his nose and stuck safety pins through his cheeks. No matter what he did though, the graduate students working with him thought it was interesting and profound. That is until the chicken bone incident.

With space to pierce at a minimum, Jackson tried to push a chicken bone through the loose skin at the bottom of his neck. The problem was that it wasn't sharp enough, or that it was too flimsy, Tommy wasn't sure which. Regardless, the end result was that the bone snapped in two and poked a hole in his trachea. They had to take him to the hospital, and the program heads had to explain to his parents that they didn't stop him because they saw value in his journey. "That's what they called it," Tommy explained with amazement showing in his eyes, "His journey."

"So what happened to the girl?" Kayla had asked between bubble gum pops.

"What girl?" Tommy said.

"You said he did it for a girl."

"I don't know if there ever was one. Maybe he was just hoping. Besides, you're missing the point."

After the hat pin cooled, Kayla went to the bathroom to retrieve a first-aid kit that was lying under a stack of Cosmopolitan magazines next to the sink. When she found it, she skipped back to the front counter and flipped it open like a magician opening a mystery chest. She had hoped to find everything one would need for home surgery, but frowned when the white aluminum case revealed only a half-full bottle of rubbing alcohol, two cotton swabs, and a few elastic bandages. She looked at Rachel leaning on her elbows from the other side of the counter, and gave a smile.

"Looks like we'll have to make do," Kayla said.

There was no one in the second-hand store, which gave the two girls all the time they needed. Sundays were the slowest days of the week so they were the best days to work. Without customers the second-hand store became their clubhouse. They would eat tofu hot dogs Kayla brought from home next to the register, and drink green tea out of bottles decorated with Aztec designs that her mother bought by the case. When their conversation died down they would dress in uniforms that had been donated and pretend to rescue one another. If no firefighter or mall security shirts had come in that week, they would have trashy fashion shows to amuse themselves, strutting up and down the long scuff-marked isles wearing prom dresses and wedding gowns that had long since served their purpose and been thrown out in the name of spring cleaning.

Cow bells hung from the front door and if they rang out a warning the girls would race back to the storeroom laughing until they couldn't breathe. Then whichever one could compose herself first would walk out front and ask the customer, "Can I help you?" It was a game, running from invading customers dressed in referee or security guard shirts that hung to their knees, but today was different. Today was serious.

"Are you ready?" Kayla asked as her hand reached out for Rachel's.

"Of course," Rachel said, noticing Kayla's manicure which today had tiny green butterflies floating against the purple painted field of each nail. The girls walked hand in hand to the back storeroom, which was cluttered with shipping boxes and plastic garbage bags filled with ratty undershirts.

Sitting on a bag full of packing peanuts, Rachel slid her pants down to her knees and leaned back onto the makeshift beanbag chair. The vent in the duct work above her blew cold air onto her face and rumbled like a milkshake machine. Looking down at her pale legs, she watched blue veins line across her thighs they way they do on the back of an old lady's hand, and wondered if someone bleeds less when they are cold. Kayla stood in front of her, stripping the packaging tape off of boxes before throwing windbreakers and suit coats to the floor.

"Are you trying to make me nervous?" Rachel asked.

"No. Wait here," Kayla said, pulling out a pair of dungarees with the knees worn through. "I want to test it first." With the jeans in hand, she folded one of the legs into a thick denim target. Then she stabbed the hat pin in to it and pulled it out quickly. "I want to make sure it's sharp enough. It has to go straight through."

"We forgot something," Rachel said as she pulled her pants back up to her hips. A knowing look came across Kayla's face, and she followed her friend back out front.

The girls walked to the front of the store singing a song neither of them could remember all the words to. At the front of the store they squatted down behind the long wooden counter, out of sight of the windows and the people on the street, next to a locked metal cabinet. Kayla took a key the color of old pennies from the cash drawer and opened the door to the cabinet. At the count of three both girls pulled on the cabinet's handle until it slowly swung open with a musty sigh.

The steel shelves inside the cabinet were stacked with boxes that might have once held baseball cards. At one time they had been white, but in the stale dusty air of the cabinet they had turned to yellow. The end of each box was marked with a permanent marker so that it was possible to know what was inside each without opening every one. The girls pulled out each box marked "Jewelry," and eased the door shut again.

Kayla sat cross-legged on the tile floor and opened the first box as Rachel scooted on her knees beside her to see what was inside. "Now you can't leave this in too long or it will turn you green. They're all fakes."

"Then why do they keep it locked up?" Rachel asked.

"I don't know," Kayla said, "Maybe some of them are real. I don't think they know one way or the other. They won't miss just one any way."

Kayla leafed through the plastic bags inside the box with a frown. The rubber jelly bracelets and glass beaded necklaces were not what she expected to find, and were completely wrong for the job.

"This box is a waste of time," she said. "Open the one over there."

Rachel picked up the box Kayla had pointed to and found much the same thing. Gaudy necklaces coiled around each other. Rings the size of drink coasters with imitation semi-precious stones heaped together like coral. Parts of wristwatches in bags like dismembered tiny robots. "This is hopeless," she said. "They should keep this junk in plastic eggs instead of baggies. They belong in a claw machine."

"Don't be sad," Kayla said. "I think I found just the thing."

Kayla hunched over a new box that sat on her lap, and pulled out another earring. "How about this?" She said.

"Don't be ridiculous," Rachel said. Kayla held up an earring that was longer than her hand.

"Just kidding," Kayla rolled her eyes. Rachel could never tell when Kayla was joking. She had the same distance of experience that her older brother had, and it made her feel young and silly. But Rachel was determined to prove that although she didn't have the benefit of a Prozac mother who didn't care what her daughter did, she could still surprise her friend.

"How about this?" Kayla asked as she held up a stud earring, but she was beginning to sound like her mom. Her mom got that same bored voice when she took the girls shopping; one that let them know it was a chore. Rachel figured Kayla wouldn't have even bothered to shop with her mom if it hadn't been the only time they spent together. All Kayla's stories involving her mom were at the mall. She said her mom liked having her around because she was young and pretty, but it also had the terrible side effect of letting her know that she wasn't anymore. "Everything with my mother has a terrible side effect," Kayla had said.

"No. Studs won't work," she said. "We need a hoop. Not too big though."

"Like this?" Kayla held up a hoop earring the size of a dime.

The girls agreed and made their way back to the storeroom after they made sure the store was still empty. It was, and they were safe.

In the storeroom the girls lifted cardboard boxes filled with winter coats and baby clothes off a Smurf blue sofa that had seen better days. When the sofa was ready, the two girls searched through the furniture that hadn't made it up front, and grabbed every lamp they could find. They found three with good bulbs, and once they were plugged in positioned them toward the sofa until it was washed in light that accentuated every cigarette burn and unidentifiable food stain on its cushions.

"Gross," Kayla said. "We need sheets."

From shipping boxes marked "Bedding" the girls pulled old hotel blankets out onto the floor. They searched through yellow sheets and bleach-spotted flannel comforters until they found a set that was snow white. They draped them over the couch which gave it a better, clinical look. "Perfect," Rachel said. With their operating room complete, the two girls turned their attention to the instruments at hand.

Kayla made sure that everything was sterilized before they got started. From the housewares isle she grabbed a punch bowl and brought it to the back along with the bottle of alcohol from the first-aid kit. She put the punch bowl on the floor, and emptied the rubbing alcohol into it before she dropped in the hat pin and earring.

"Now at least you won't end up like Katie did," Kayla said.

"Right," Rachel said. "I'd rather die."

Katie was a girl they had known in middle school. Her mom was so strict that she had forbidden her from getting her ears pierced, so she did it herself one night at a sleepover with a sewing needle. She didn't know to clean the needle, or was in too much of a hurry to consider things like that, and ended up with a fungus that turned her ears the color of orange creamcicles for almost a year.

"What ever happened to her?" Rachel asked as she stood.

"Who knows?" Kayla answered. "Let's just let this sit for awhile."

Rachel looked down at the pin sitting in the punch bowl, and for the first time took in the fact that it was no longer a game. She had liked the idea, but wondered what the reality of going through with it would do to her. She set herself, and resolved to go through with it no matter what out of fear that she would never live it down if she backed out. If she got scared and quit she would stay two steps behind everyone she knew for the rest of her life, and she hated the idea of being like a kid sister to girls her own age. For once she would be the first, and girls like Kayla would have to follow her lead.

"I'm ready," Rachel said. "I just want to go to the bathroom first in case." Kayla shrugged, and sat on the floor where she spun the bowl around to watch the pin dance.

Rachel peed and read the same issues of Teen People that she had a dozen times before. Its gloss was gone, replaced by the mean comments Kayla wrote over the faces of models and pop stars. The things Kayla had written in magazines had made her laugh before, but now only added to her nerves. There was no way for her to tell if Kayla was helping her to be a friend, or just to see what it would be like. Rachel didn't want to turn into one of Kayla's horror stories, but she was stuck. When she finished Kayla came in and washed her hands. It was time to get started.

In the store outside, Kayla pulled a V-neck nurse's smock patterned with hurt teddy bears over her tank top. The girls laughed as she was the first nurse either of them had ever seen with a nose ring.

"What do you think?" Kayla said as she modeled her uniform.

"You look like a pro," Rachel said.

Since no one had bothered to visit the store all day the girls got brave. Kayla stood on a step stool so that she could reach the stereo, then pushed in a CD she'd gotten from the boy she was secretly dating who was in a college band. The boy who Rachel had never met was further proof that Kayla was far more advanced than herself. When the music started to play Kayla turned the volume up as loud as it would go until it was nearly impossible for either girl to think.

"It sounds like a trash can falling down a stairwell!" Rachel shouted as she covered her ears.

"Noise rock!" Kayla yelled back as she jumped around. "Don't you know about it?"

After a minute the music became too much to take. Rachel pointed at the stereo, and Kayla shut it off.

"It's time," Rachel said.

"This way," Kayla said as she put her arm around her friend. "I've been expecting you."

In the storeroom the instruments were laid out on a clean white T-shirt that had a Red Cross emblem sewn onto the pocket. The hat pin sat next to a wash cloth and the earring shined like new. Rachel took her place on the couch as Kayla fished around in the pockets of her jeans for a treat.

"Take these first," she said as she handed her two robin egg blue pills. "They always help my mom relax." Rachel swallowed the pills dry, and sank back into the cushions. She closed her eyes closed, and could hear the sound of her heartbeat. After a deep breath she pulled her pants off and kicked them to the side.

Kayla played up being a nurse by checking her friend's pulse as her chest rose and fell in the steady rhythm of someone searching for peace. She adjusted the lights positioned above, and put on opera gloves, which were the best substitute for real latex surgical ones she could find.

"Before we do this," Rachel said, "I want to make sure I will be the first."

"You will be," Kayla said, her voice softening. "I promise." The girls listed everyone at their school who had their belly buttons pierced, every person with a lip ring or surgical steel ball sticking out of their cheek, until they were satisfied that it was true.

"You need to take those off," Kayla whispered and pointed at Rachel's panties. They said "Wednesday," but she had learned a long time ago that no one ever wore the ones with the right day on them.

"You're right," Rachel said, then stopped with a new idea that might save her. "What if we did my boob instead?"

"In Jamaica my sister says it costs almost two-hundred dollars to get your boobs pierced and that doesn't include tip," Kayla said. "You have to tip for everything there, even toilet paper."

"We're not in Jamaica," Rachel said.

"OK, but a junior girl got hers done last week. I heard her mom signed and everything. Plus you don't want to end up like Eli."

"Who's Eli?" Rachel asked.

"This kid I know," Kayla said, sliding closer. "He got it worse than anyone." Her eyes turned white as grains of minute rice and her cheeks glowed as if she had a mouth full of juicy fruit. It was the look of pure delight she had every time she began one of her suburban horror stories.

"Eli pierced his own nipple, but he went too deep or something," she said. "It always got infected so he had to take it out. When he did it left this BB of scar tissue that looked like a third nipple, right? Well one night he was picking at it when he was really high and it came off, but there was this string attached. He sat and flipped the string for awhile, but it wouldn't come off. So he took a pair of scissors and cut the string. The next day he woke up in the hospital. It wasn't a string after all, but like some nerve that attached to his heart. He had a heart attack right? No lie." Kayla smiled wider as she tugged Rachel's panties to the floor. Then she picked up the pin. "Just chill okay?"

There was no way to get comfortable on the couch since every way Rachel moved pushed her bare ass into a different spring or the wooden frame. With Kayla's help, she lifted her right leg into position on the arm rest and began to breathe the way she was taught to in yoga class. For a second the room got quiet, and neither girl moved.

Kayla pinched the folds between Rachel's thighs together, and the veins on her legs turned blue as ice packs. It felt like she had swallowed a snowball, and could feel it running down the center of her body.

"Hold it." Kayla whispered over the sound of her friend pushing the air out of her lungs. "Hold it."

When the pin pierced her, the snowball inside Rachel turned into a flame. She bit through her lip as she felt it pull back out, and the earring hook her hood. It took only a second before it was done. She was left electrified, unable to move. Blood filled her mouth with copper, and the center of her body felt like she'd sat on a knife. Kayla stared up at her with glassy jealous eyes.

"Promise not to tell," Rachel said when she could speak again. She felt suddenly older, and knew she had passed the test.

"Of course," Kayla said as she covered Rachel's legs with a beach towel. "See how much I love you."

The two girls hugged one another as the bells on the front door rang.

What They Don't Tell You

You drive your van to the house on your service call sheet and try not to hurry. There's no reason to hurry. Every call is given a five hour window to wait for you to appear. The people are nice to you when you arrive. They open the doors, put their little barking dogs away, and show you where the television is. Then they hide. They disappear into upstairs bedrooms, clomp down basement steps, or if the weather is warm, putter around their gardens until you leave. They can't rest with you in the house. They won't help you move their furniture so you can get to the wires, or tell you how they've rigged their home theater systems. You have to figure that out for yourself. The cable company never warns you about this in training; that you will feel more like a burglar than a service tech when you go out on calls.

I have come to accept it. With no one watching me I take my time. I walk around the client's living rooms and am surprised by the bad taste that surrounds me: homes that look like unlivable Pier One showrooms with empty vases, homes with motley yarn art pictures of big-eyed owls, framed commemorative plates of civil war battles. I've seen it all. Eventually I'll go to work and add a new receiver. Eventually. My wife says I need to take my job more seriously.

America revolves around dumb jobs. I used to make balloon animals at birthday parties. I hated filing my taxes. Occupation: Clown. Kids would scream, "Make me a dinosaur!" or "I want an elephant now!" Everything I made looked like a dick to me. The party company never bothered to warn me about taking requests. Eventually enough mothers complained.

After failing at the clown racket, I got a job with the cable company. I took service calls from people who didn't know their sets were unplugged, from wives who were shocked at the things their husbands had ordered on pay-per-view. I'd offer my advice. People offered my supervisor theirs. After a few months they put me out in the field to be safe. My wife said I was proving her mother right.

You screw the cable into the cable box, and then take the wire from the box to the television. You patch in the VCR and the DVD player. You coordinate the remote control so all the buttons work. This is your contribution to society. No one bothers to check in on you. They hate that they need you in the first place.

I've started to pocket collectable saltshakers before I yell for the clients to come see their new eight hundred channels offering movies, cartoons, sports, news, and weather updates by the minute. I slide magazines I haven't read into my jacket, pull fresh fruit off kitchen tables and toss them in my toolkit, and am building a nice collection of coffee mugs. I snag anniversary presents from night stands, Sweetest Day gifts hidden in the basement, prescription bottles from medicine cabinets to make the time go.

    Little gifts make a marriage run smoothly. The clients are plugged in; tuned out. Things at home are coming along. My tax form says technician now, and my wife says I'm so thoughtful.

Swimmers

Denise

Collapsed on a rose-colored couch, under a black and white print of children exchanging bouquets, Denise soaked her feet in saltwater and waited to be appalled by the cruelty of nature. According to the entertainment section of the newspaper she had already missed a documentary about a boy who had been born with two heads, and a countdown show featuring the *One Hundred and One Most Bizarre Self-Inflicted Injuries*. This left her with only the last half-hour of *The Eight-Hundred-Pound Man* before she began her ritual. She rubbed the soles of her feet together in the lukewarm water and tried to muster a sob.

It seemed impossible to Denise that a man who weighed more

than eight-hundred pounds could play an instrument, but as she watched he strummed a guitar on his stomach while a nurse at his side hummed along. Denise inched the volume up until she could almost make out the tune of "Every Rose Has Its Thorn." The medical staff brought a hydraulic lift to the man's bedside. Orderlies gently moved his guitar off-screen while they positioned themselves to the sides of his limbs, readying straps in place before the commercial break.

Denise sat silent as a commercial for newly-solved medical mysteries played, and prayed that the man would survive the show. She had witnessed narrated reports of deaths off-screen before, and hoped this program would end with a soft-focus shot of the man walking hand in hand with a loved one through the park. She had to hope that some medical impossibility could be solved, that people like herself could be saved, or else there would be no point in believing in the promise of tomorrow.

When the program returned, the narrator gave ominous warnings about the eight-hundred-pound man's circulation and escalating diabetes. While he addressed the audience at home, the man's sister wept in a hallway as an emergency surgery was conducted to correct the giant's deficient heart. At this, Denise turned the television off and hoped that angels would intercede on the man's behalf, but feared that they wouldn't for the sake of drama. She dried her pedicured toes with a dish towel in front of the television, pleased that she had found her pity for the night.

A failing body is a private temple. Nightmares of television crews had visited Denise. Cameras would light in the dark of her apartment and pan across the baby magazines lying on her floor. Print ads of smiling children, of pregnant women in bikinis, were illuminated for the audience at home. The steady voice of a narrator came from the ether, begging of her "Why don't you have children?" Boom mikes dangled like nooses in front of her face. In her sleep she whispered, "I am trying," before the lights engulfed her. In her quiet room she could hear the film turning on reels until she was shaken awake, suddenly alone.

When the dream came and evaporated, she knew that television cameras would never find her. She was a medical oddity too common to consider past prime time.

But for Denise there was community in the world for the childless, and it was this sisterhood that she prepared for each night with cable shorts about plastic surgery disasters and children born allergic to water. Only when she was filled with sympathy, when tears for strangers crowded the corners of her eyes, could she join women like herself online to post updates about Polycystic Ovarian Syndrome or uterine linings too thin to hold an egg.

"Soul-Cysters" was a website for women like Denise. On it they posted updates about drug treatments while their husbands slept. They wrote down all the things the men in their lives couldn't hope to understand. They cried together, and promised to meet on a day when all their children would play in the sun and be photographed for parenting magazines. They dreamed together when fertility clinics had given up hope.

If Denise hadn't herself worked at a fertility clinic, if she hadn't seen so many women like her flip through the pages of baby catalogues they would never use, she wouldn't have needed the television. But the years had stripped the pity from her, leaving her to watch documentaries about conjoined twins or shark attack victims before she could log on. She understood if she couldn't grieve, if even for herself, there was no place for her in the world.

Fox

Fox watched the sports report alone in bed while the dog he envied greatly ignored him. His dog was a cock-a-poo, the result of suburban science's efforts to minimize everything masculine in the world. When he looked down at his dog casually licking his paws clean he saw the great progression of dogs running wild in the forest tearing apart deer, to dogs taught to beg for peanut butter flavored bones and mouth "I love you" by housewives, all the way down to dogs like his own who were woolly mild-mannered things afraid of laundry baskets. His dog was evidence of the hands of women shrinking the wildness of the world into cute packages they could shoo away.

At that moment he never felt closer to the dog he named Whiskey to annoy his wife. Together they lived in a home neither of them owned, and kept to themselves to avoid the tasks his wife might assign them. They had been domesticated.

Whiskey was a stop-gap measure, a stand-in until his wife had a child. They got him a year ago when the night stand next to their bed held sex toys and lube. Now an ovulation kit that measured his wife's hormone levels was in the night stand on top of pamphlets for artificial insemination. Nothing killed his sex drive like her baby addiction, and he couldn't remember the last time they'd had sex. Even when they did she had to spit and check her hormones first which left him half-hard at best. Most times he'd hurry through so that he could finish himself off in the bathroom after she thought he'd came in her. Fox watched Whiskey roll onto his back and grin, completely unaware that the world around him was heading south.

"Are you coming to bed?" Fox called down the hall, as he absently scratched Whiskey's belly. Only the sound of keystrokes answered as he switched off the lamp.

Before dreaming, Fox imagined his wife having a lurid affair over the internet with a man who wouldn't appreciate her. He saw himself coming home one day to find only the dog and a note from his wife detailing how he never supported her. On that day he would move to Tahiti or some other sunny foreign place, and begin a new life full of afternoon flings with women who spoke broken English. In that world before sleep, he saw himself drinking in rum bars where women who wore next to nothing would push his head into their breasts and coo, "I want you." He could picture himself walking along the beach with the only person who understood him off his leash. In that world they were unbound.

Greta

Down the hall, Fox's wife Greta was exploring her own dream world, one warmed by the glow of motherhood. At her desk it occurred to her that a voice had called for her several minutes before, but by the time it came to her it was only an echo. Bent over the keyboard she had been too involved to answer.

Taking a moment to stare down the hall toward her bedroom, she glanced to see if the light was still on but found only the indigo glow of a muted television flickered in the dark. She made a note to apologize in the morning and posted it to the side of her monitor, the yellow square adding to her regret.

"If he only knew what it feels like to be empty," she thought. "If he cared that he couldn't do what he was meant to..." This was a familiar refrain; one she no longer bothered to share.

Her train of thought derailed, Greta slid her hand underneath envelopes holding electric bills and mortgage statements until she found the pencil box she kept hidden. Inside it were three cigarettes. With one in hand she quietly walked down the stairs to find matches before easing out the back door of her home. She lit a menthol as she sat in a folding chair on the lawn, and watched the blue glow from the bedroom above her shimmer while she reclined alone with her secret.

Fox believed she had given up smoking a year and a half ago. He also believed that she was happy, and that having a child was a financial decision. When he found her sobbing over baby clothes in department stores, he would frown and tell her how rich they were. That they should be grateful they didn't live like African refugees or the poverty-stricken families they saw in charity ads. But for Greta, the opinion of a man who couldn't tell a crib from a cradle offered no comfort. The doctor said she was the picture of health, and this left only Fox to blame.

Staring into the smoke trails that lifted in the breeze, she saw the great progression of her life from a child beauty queen, to a Phi Beta Kappa student landing a rewarding asset manager position. She had achieved so much by twenty-eight. Only bearing a child was left to do, and her life would be complete. But nature was against her. She watched her wedding day swirl in the smoke trails above her, and disappear in the night.

In the kitchen she washed her face and hands to remove the scent of mint and tobacco; then she made her way to the bed where the men in her life lay asleep. Under the covers she watched muted television spots for third world relief agencies featuring starving women with swaddled children in their arms. She envied them.

Denise

Behind the glass of the waiting room's office, Denise rubbed the sleep out of her eyes and turned the radio to a classical music station. Across from her a young couple sat on plastic furniture whispering to one another.

The young woman struggled to smile and reassured the tired-eyed man sitting next to her, explaining things Denise couldn't hear. Realizing they were being watched, the young woman turned her attention to a childcare magazine, and the man slumped down in his seat, pulling his baseball cap down over his eyes.

Denise watched as the young man's feet bounced against the floor like a school boy about to receive a booster shot. She had seen hundreds of men like him pass by the glass in front of her reception desk, and knew that a semen analysis was the closest a man could come to understanding how she felt. Sometimes these men would sit on their hands or pace from one end of the waiting room to the other with worry naked on their faces. Would they be able to perform? Would their count be high enough? Their number was beyond their control. If it was too low, would they still be men?

The young woman signed for the man she introduced as her husband, and Denise led them to a room down the hall with a plastic cup in hand. As the man entered the room dropped-shouldered, Denise smiled faintly at his wife.

"I'm sure everything will be fine," she said. "These things just take time."

"We've been trying for almost a year," the young woman said coldly.

"Some people struggle for years before it happens. We had a patient last month who got pregnant after six." Denise began to feel as if she was speaking to the door as much as to the client standing next to her checking her watch.

"You know the worst part?" The young woman asked, her hand pressed against the wall. "I hope it's his fault. I really hope he is the reason. It sounds terrible, but if it's him I can find someone else." Tears inched down her soft cheeks. "I've found matches you know, from restaurants we've never been to." The young woman pulled matchbooks from her purse and held them up for Denise to see. "I still have them."

Denise took a tissue out of her smock and led the woman back to the waiting room, inside hoping that the husband was the reason as well. She thought about how men don't have the same aching for children that women do, and she hated them for that.

After a few minutes passed, the young man returned to the waiting room and sat down next to his wife. She whispered questions to him, her hands motioning for details he couldn't supply as if he could judge the quality of his sample by holding it up to the light. Denise watched quietly as they worked out their positions on where they were together, and when the mood cooled she scheduled a follow up appointment with a polite smile. As the couple walked toward the door, she passed pamphlets to the young woman covering in-vitro fertilization and adoption services.

Damir

Denise returned to the room to retrieve the young man's sample. She walked quickly down the hallway leading to the lab, and hoped no one would stop her to make small-talk since the fresher the sample the higher the count.

In the lab she thumbed a label onto the plastic cup, and handed it to a lab tech named Damir who had once asked to kiss her. He had asked so earnestly and desperately that Denise was left no chance at offense. She could only stare back in confusion while the man tried to explain himself in a way she could understand.

"You have to know," Damir had pleaded, "If I kiss you now I will be free. I can leave my wife and be with another woman. I will have crossed over." He had looked at her as if he had expected something she couldn't imagine.

Standing in her comfortable shoes, with her simple glasses and her hair pinned back, she must have looked incredibly plain. When the memory comes to her, Denise pictures herself dressed as a nun standing with her back against the sink listening to Damir's confession as he stammers to make sense.

"My wife," he continued, "I could never cheat on her. I wouldn't know how. If I do one small thing like this, then I will know."

When Damir remembers this moment, on the nights he drinks alone in his car before coming home, he imagines Denise flirting with him. She uses her beauty to torture him. She wanted a child. It was no secret. She would destroy him for a child. In memory he pushes Denise away as she struggles to kiss him, and is proud of himself. He knows he is a good man.

The kiss never came, and that day in the cramped lab seems as impossibly distant to both of them at this moment in time as their kindergarten graduation or their first word.

"Just one," Damir asked, as he took the sample from Denise.

"Yes. It's still warm."

"Maybe he is a swimmer."

"I don't think so," Denise said. "We haven't had a swimmer in seven months."

Romance for Delinquents

Fox

At thirty years old, Fox felt he was too young for a mid-life crisis. But as he edged the volume of his stereo up as far as he could without causing a migraine, he had to wonder what direction his life was taking. Wearing pajama pants and a Motorhead T-shirt, sitting on the floor of his guest room unshaven and bored, he felt much the same as he had when he was a thirteen-years-old. The only difference was that instead of his mother, the door to his room shut out the evidence of the woman he had promised to love for the rest of his life. He watched the numbers on the clock tick down to the time when Greta would return, and danced around the room with his arms in the air. His life for the next hour would be on his terms.

The decision had come early in the morning. A scratch in his throat gave birth to the idea that he was dangerously under the weather and shouldn't show up for work. With his best raw-neck voice he phoned a personnel secretary at the management office where he worked and told her of his plight. Then he began to drink beers one after another until only the music existed. Greta had gone to work and to the doctor, moving through the routines that got her what she wanted, leaving him alone to appreciate the pleasantness of being properly drunk in the afternoon as the rest of the world moved on completely unaware.

He had spent the morning reading yearbooks filled with people he could hardly remember. The pictures were awkward caricatures of youth with hairstyles as outdated as his CD collection. He toasted his former classmates, and wondered if he called them at home to ask them what they did with their lives how many would answer with the number of children they had. This only made him drink more, until he shouted at the pages, "Go to Denmark before you die!" or "Steal a car to see how it feels!"

By four in the afternoon the yearbooks were scattered on the bedroom floor, and Fox was considering getting a tattoo of an eagle fighting a tiger. This thought dissolved in a haze as the garage door clattered open. His time was up.

Greta made her way up the stairs to find her husband on the floor next to a stereo blaring incomprehensible British metal. It was not the homecoming she had hoped for.

"You didn't go to work today?" she asked.

"No," Fox replied.

"How did you spend your day?"

"Spent."

Fox lifted himself off the floor and made his way to the bathroom in hopes that she wouldn't bother to follow, or want to talk. In the bathtub he tried to remember the last time they had sex for the fun of it, when there was no hint of her agenda.

"You can't do this anymore," Greta said as she watched her husband's head disappear underneath the water every time she spoke.

"I know."

"No, you're not listening. No drinking for the next three days." Again his head played submarine.

"It was a day for drink. What can I say?"

"No. Three days. You have to give a sample," Greta said as calmly as she could manage.

"You want my blood?" Fox asked, and he flopped one arm over the side of the tub.

"No," Greta answered, as she tossed the only dry towel in the bathroom into the tub. "Not a blood sample."

Denise

Denise ate frozen yogurt, as a calm voice from her television screen catalogued all the species of roses that had disappeared from the planet during the last decade, and wondered if swimmers were quickly becoming extinct as well. A true swimmer hadn't dropped off a sample at the fertility clinic in months. This shouldn't have been remarkable, since like scarce varieties of tropical tea roses they seemed to spring from the most unexpected place then disappear forever, but their absence frustrated Denise all the more. The world was drying up. Swimmers were growing extinct.

The average human sperm count is around twenty million sperm per milliliter with about half of those active. Most of the men who came to the fertility clinic were either at or below that number. Every now and then though, a man would leave a sample that was extraordinary. A man like that was referred to by the lab techs as a "swimmer."

A swimmer could have up to forty or fifty million sperm per sample and up to ninety percent of those would be active. Under a microscope his sperm would look like a crowded ant colony on crystal meth. The reason men like these were deemed swimmers though had nothing to do with the amount of writhing sperm they left behind.

According to Damir, the term went back to Greg Louganis. Urban legend among lab techs had it that Greg Louganis had donated sperm in the early nineties in California, and that his counts were so high that from the day he left the clinic forward all men with incredible sperm counts would be known as "swimmers."

When Damir explained the rational for the term to Denise it seemed perfectly reasonable and impossible at the same time. It made sense in that Greg Louganis was a multi-medal winning Olympic athlete. Fitness in the scientific sense is the ability to reproduce. But to Denise medals alone couldn't be an honest indicator that a man's Speedo held the fertility of the Nile Valley. It also bothered her that Greg Louganis was a diver after all, and not a swimmer.

In the end she accepted the myth as truth, just as she had accepted in high school that the "Jumping Jack" was named after Jack Lalanne. Stranger things had happened, and were recreated to shock home audiences every night.

With the taste of sugar bringing on the guilt of an unused gym membership, Denise watched the last Steputis tea rose get crushed under the tracks of a Brazilian logging company's bulldozer. When the petals of the flower were only white flakes on the ground, she turned off her television and returned to the website to update strangers about the status of her womb. It was easier to share her feelings with strangers since unlike her mother they didn't bother her by recommending men who were newly divorced.

Romance for Delinquents

On her computer screen she viewed pictures of women older than herself who were entering their third trimester. She scrolled through the photos of sloping mid-sections, and tried to post comments of encouragement. The fact that the women's age heightened the risk of autism she kept to herself. She had gotten angry messages in the past when she volunteered the sad truths she knew too well. Instead, she wrote about how thrilled she was for the expectant mothers, and wished that she lived closer to Kansas, or Oregon, or Montana, or wherever else they happened to live. If she only lived closer, she posted, they could meet for coffee or shop for baby clothes together. She had to be excited for the pregnant few. It was the only hope she saw that nature, sometimes, changed its mind.

The women who posted had an advantage Denise wished desperately for. They had men in their lives who could grant them children when the stars in the sky and the hormones in their bloodstreams aligned. Denise had to make do with men she met in dance clubs on the weekend or through online dating services; men who could be married, and posed more danger than promise. It was another regret she would not share with her mother, but a necessary one. To these men she was a body, one they believed to be on birth control. To Denise these men were nameless donors who had yet to succeed in changing her life for the better. The empty yogurt container mocked her efforts to stay beautiful for the nameless men who visited her when the longing became too much to bear.

Before bed Denise prayed for her body to realign itself in the night. She prayed for the cysts on her ovaries to break loose like kidney stones and roll down her bed sheets. She prayed for the swimmers to return.

Fox

Fox surveyed his surroundings as his feelings of hopelessness grew. Sitting on a plastic chair that reminded him of the furniture in a dorm lobby, he tried to collect himself. Half-awake in the cold room, he had never felt less sexual in his life. He could hear the sound of his wife pacing just outside the door. The plastic cup mocked him.

A clock on the wall counted away the minutes, and he wondered how soon it would be before he could leave. If he left too soon would he be a joke? If he took too long would his wife shrug her shoulders at the pretty nurse who had escorted him to the room, and would they both laugh? He pictured his wife checking her watch and wondering what was taking so long, but what did she expect so early in the morning?

While the secondhand clicked with a water torture pace, Fox took in his surroundings. The walls were drab and unadorned. The floor was tile for easy cleaning. Paper flowers collected dust on an end table in the corner, and nothing seemed meant to inspire the lurid behavior that was required of him. A television set sat quietly on top of an entertainment system with a VCR in front of the chair. It was his only hope.

The selection of videos did not make him feel any better. They were outdated tapes of bleach blonde overly-tanned women with claw like fingernails and muscle bound middle-aged men groping one another to bad dance music by swimming pools or in cheap office settings. They were tacky familiar scenarios he was too tired to work himself into, and they only made him want to get out of the room as soon as possible. But taking off without getting off wasn't an option since it would lead to arguments he couldn't win. He had to perform.

Fox rolled his neck a few times, pulled down his pants, and got his game face on. He cleared his head and let Greta, the bad porn, and the plastic cup disappear. He wasn't old. He didn't need to grow up or get serious like Greta always said. He looked down at his penis, and knew he was still a machine. His hand stroked it hard. He told himself he was a winner, and thought of all the college girls he'd had before Greta made him get serious. He saw their legs spread and waiting for him, their twenty-year-old asses bent over his bed. He imagined Greta watching him fuck them in front of her out of spite. Tension ran up his spine as he pointed his hard on toward the cup and stroked faster. The cup became a sorority girl's mouth begging for him to finish while his wife was forced to watch. His body jerked as he came harder than he had in months.

When he was done he sealed the cup the way he had been shown, and put it by the fake flowers on the table. Then he left the room and walked to the parking lot without saying a word to Greta or the nurse who watched him pass through the waiting room.

On the drive home Greta noticed he seemed to take it all better than she thought, and was glad. She missed the feeling that they were a team.

"So was there anything worth watching in there?" she asked.

"No," Fox said as he looked out the window. "I had to use my imagination."

"What'd you come up with?"

"Only you," Fox said. "It was all about you." He knew he'd never come back for another test no matter how much she begged him. She had what she wanted, and if it wasn't enough to make her happy again he hoped she'd let him go.

Damir

Damir's wife Irena sat at the table of their condominium reading a gossip magazine. She had brought it home with her from the drugstore where she had gone to get a flu shot. "They gave me the shot for half-price," she had told her husband. "I said I was pregnant. There is a discount if you are pregnant." Damir stood in the corner and watched her disappear into the pictures of beautiful people. He saw how careful she was not to crease the pages or tear the corners. She seemed to have forgotten him so quickly. He had walked to the bathroom after dinner, and when he returned she had the magazine and he felt like a memory.

"It is a shame the way these people live," Irena said.

"What people?" Damir asked, as he worked the cap off of a bottle of cough syrup.

"The ones who get divorced in Hollywood. The rich ones," Irena said.

Damir put down the cough syrup bottle for a moment and placed his hands on his wife's shoulders. "Irena, you should come to bed now before I get tired."

"Do you think I should go on a diet?" Irena asked.

"Why do you ask?"

"This one here," Irena said pointing at a picture of a woman with huge sunglasses and a floppy hat, "she went on a diet and lost twenty pounds in one month. Not just water."

"Do you think a diet would change you?" Damir asked as he drank the cough syrup slowly.

"What do you mean change me?" Irena asked as she closed the magazine on the table top. "I need to change?"

Damir shook his head slowly and drank again from the cough syrup bottle, the thick cherry flavor filling his throat and promising him sleep. "We all look for it," he said, then walked to the bedroom alone.

Under the sheets of his bed, Damir listened to the blades of an oscillating fan in the corner skittering dust. The cough syrup failed him and he lay in bed restless. He saw the man he was growing older by the minute, eroding like a shoreline. He heard the echoes of women from the clinic talking about the children that would come to them, the sound of his wife ordering jewelry from the television in whispers over the phone, and the laughs of waitresses talking about the men who would deliver them happiness. Everyone searched for change.

His mind pulled him awake, backwards in time to a vision of himself smoking cigarettes in a tavern and crashing into the bodies of young women on warm summer nights. In the vision he was an eager university student who only believed in passion. The man he was left the tavern and walked down the sidewalk as street lamps shut off. The road ahead darkened as he walked toward his future.

Greta

Greta folded white undershirts next to a stack of pressed khaki pants, then arranged them on the bedspread by a neat row of rolled up dress socks and folded boxer shorts. She moved a pair of dress shoes and a pair of sneakers next to the suitcase where it sat on the floor, and checked the contents of her husband's overnight bag to ensure that there was enough toothpaste to get him through the week. If she let Fox pack for himself she knew that he would inevitably end up with eight stained undershirts, a pair of underwear and no socks, so she took it on herself to ensure that he had everything that he would need for his time away. It wasn't a divorce. It was a pause.

When his things were in order, she loaded his suitcase and leaned it against the bed next to his shoes and jacket. Some men go on fishing trips when the world bears down too heavily on their shoulders. Others leave without any notice and blow through their 401(k)s in Las Vegas. She took comfort in the fact that at least she knew where her husband would be staying, and that their bank accounts were all in her name.

With the packing finished, Greta retouched her make-up in the guest bathroom as the sound of a football game rumbled up the stairs. Rosewater perfume wafted in the air from the nape of her neck. She would let him talk about himself. She would give him the time to change his mind.

In the living room, Fox sat in a recliner and pouted. He had hardly spoken since they returned from the clinic, and looked like something had been taken from him. This was something Greta could almost forgive, as she knew how it felt to be examined, had he made the slightest effort to talk about it with her. The results from his semen analysis hadn't even come in yet, but he'd still developed some grudge against her for no reason she could see.

"You have everything you need," Greta said. "I only ask that you give me a call when you get to the hotel. I've made your reservation."

"Reservations," Fox answered.

"What do you hope to gain from this? Honestly, I don't understand how living two miles away for a week is going to bring any enlightenment."

"I'm not looking for enlightenment. I just want to breathe." The volume on the television grew louder, as the thunder from a football game mixed with the sound of children playing in the street.

"You can breathe here can't you? I'm not asking for your soul. I just want you to be there for me. This is something we are doing together."

"This is the life you want."

"And what do you want?" Greta asked, as she counted out twenty-dollar bills from her purse and stacked them neatly in an envelope.

"I haven't decided yet. I haven't been given the chance."

"That's not true and you know it. We've talked about this for over a year."

"I've listened."

"Some day you will look back at this and smile."

Fox raised himself off the recliner and took the envelope from Greta's hand without bothering to count the allowance she had portioned out for his escape.

"Does the hotel allow dogs?"

"No."

Fox walked to the kitchen, carrying Whiskey in his arms. Under his breath he shared secrets with the furry mound, but Greta could only hear the sound of his footsteps moving away. "He will have his way," she thought. "This is only for a week."

In the living room, Fox placed his hand on Greta's shoulder and nudged their dog closer to her legs with his foot. He promised to call when he reached his retreat, five minutes away.

When he was gone Greta lit a cigarette in the living room and inhaled the taste of mint leaves and smog. Whiskey had apparently forgotten about his master and was busy chewing his way through a rubber ball. She sat on the floor and accepted the fact that smoking could hamper her fertility. She took a long slow drag, and blamed Fox's childishness for endangering the little hope she had left.

Damir

For the majority of the morning, Damir had sat alone on a metal stool in the lab drinking flat soda and considering his options. He had no gift for lying so he imagined himself an actor. When the time came, he would leave his body and play the role just as he had envisioned it.

He would watch the production play out with the same casual indifference his wife showed toward her daily soap operas. It was his only hope of success. One must not seem eager for an act as dull and common as procreation, for if one does, it becomes painfully obvious that the physical collision is only a desire—the emotion which seemed to distress Americans the most.

The lunch hour came and went. Through the slats of the Venetian blinds at his window, he watched cars leave the clinic parking lot and return. Women who worked in medical records returned with Styrofoam to-go boxes. Men from the geriatrics office upstairs drank coffee by the entrance and talked. To work, to lunch, to work, to home; the people that surrounded him each day seemed to have no appreciation for life at all. They had whittled their time down to routine. They were mechanical. He would be mechanical too.

By two-thirty in the afternoon the office was empty. Appointments were rarely made outside of lunch breaks or morning hours that could be counted as half-days off. Alone with the echoes of his shoes falling onto the waxed tile floor, Damir made his way to the waiting room to begin his performance.

He parted his hair on the other side of his brow at a water fountain in the hallway, unbuttoned his shirt collar, and admired himself in the reflection of the faucet head. The beard he had worn since his twenties was gone, revealing pallid gray skin. The eyebrows which had brushed out like worn brooms had been trimmed and dyed. "If my wife could see me now," he thought, "she would not know me."

With a casual stride he modeled after George Clooney, Damir

ambled up to the front desk where Denise was listening quietly to Chopin while she mused over a word for revolution with seven letters.

"Denise," he said. "If you have the time, I would like to speak with you. I have something to show you. I think you will be surprised." Inside he held the test results from the man who came in the day before. Only the name had been changed. He would be a swimmer for her.

Denise pulled the ink pen from her mouth, giving up on the crossword puzzle which had frustrated her for the last hour, and walked to meet the man she hardly recognized outside.

Greta

When the news came Greta was in the car before the nurse on the other end of the call finished speaking. Through the receiver Greta heard the woman desperately trying to ensure that she appreciated how incredibly rare the results were, but she was deaf. She threw her cell phone onto the backseat of her Navigator and raced down the street ignoring both stop signs and crosswalks. Later, she wouldn't remember driving to the hotel at all.

Greta parked her car in the fire lane at the side of the hotel, and ran through the lobby trying her best not to shout in ecstasy. Once in the elevator she arranged her auburn hair behind her ears, and smoothed out her dress. The numbers above the door lit up and fell dull as she ascended up toward the executive floor where she had reserved a room for her husband. Alone in the elevator, she slid her thong down her legs and tucked it into her purse. She only prayed that Fox's depression hadn't lifted; that instead of going to a stupid sports bar he was still moping in bed.

In the hall Greta kicked off her shoes before knocking on the door. There was no answer at first, but as she slapped her palms against the door she could hear rumbling inside. Fox answered the door in his underwear with three days worth of stubble showing on his square jaw. His eyes flashed pink in the light of the hallway.

"What are you doing here?" he said.

"You're wonderful!" Greta shouted. "It was all bad timing. That's all!" With that she pushed passed him, closed the door, and ducked into the bathroom.

"I am wonderful," Fox repeated, as he crashed back onto the bed. "What's all this?"

In the bathroom, Greta touched up her lipstick and searched her purse for a thermometer before discovering that in her haste she had left it at home. She took a deep breath to calm herself as the television in the next room moved from one channel to another. She undid the buttons on her blouse and took off her bra before leaving the bathroom to walk half-naked to the foot of the bed.

"Fox I have some amazing news," she said as she sat on sheets that smelled like sweat and Chinese take-out.

"Did you get a promotion?" he asked without taking his eyes off the set.

"Why would you say that?"

"You seem like the kind of person who would get one."

"I didn't come here to talk about money. I got my test results back today, your test results." Greta slid closer to Fox and lifted her breasts toward his face like trophies, hoping he would at least drop the remote control.

"Am I dying?" he asked.

"What are you talking about?"

"I fell asleep with the television on last night. It was on one of the music channels. When I woke up this morning I saw that I'd been listening to soft rock all night."

"Soft rock?" she arched herself closer so that her breasts covered half of his face. He could talk about whatever he wanted if he came to her.

"The thing is, and I can't be sure of this, I think I was enjoying it." He put his hand on her breast and softly rubbed its nipple with his thumb. "Am I old?"

"You need to listen to me," Greta said as she took the remote control from his hand, "I'm trying to tell you something."

"I hate soft rock."

"I hate soft rock too," Greta nuzzled her face into his neck, and began to take wet licks against the stubble she found there. Her hand moved underneath his boxers to stroke him. "You are amazing."

"I miss this," Fox said.

Greta stripped his boxers off, and lifted her skirt up to straddle him. She rocked her ass slowly until he stiffened fully under her. With her eyes fixed down onto his sad child face she said, "You are my husband."

"Your has-been," Fox smiled up with a sneer.

Greta lifted up her hips, and guided his swollen penis inside her. "I want you!"

Fox gripped her hips as she bucked against him and clawed his arms like a teenage dream. She seemed so much younger. "Tell me I'm special."

"You are," she said as her breath sped up. "You're so special."

Denise

Denise could hear water running from the faucet in the bathroom and feared that the bath was dangerously close to overflowing. It was a silly thing to be concerned with given her present circumstances, but as she lay naked on the bed she allowed her mind to wander over the small details that surrounded her. There were pamphlets for local attractions stacked neatly on the night stand, and a phone book half-visible from the drawer cracked open underneath. Outside the window she could hear the sounds of car stereos and the chirp of crosswalks. The chocolates which had been carefully arranged on the pillows now lay on the floor by her dress.

As she came back into herself, she allowed her palms to move over the cold flesh of her stomach until they rested beneath her belly button. Rising up on her elbows, she stared at her belly under the tangerine glow cast from the lamp.

Water met water and sounded out peacefully as if there was a stream flowing in the adjoining bathroom. She could hear Damir moving underneath that tide from the faucet. With contentment and a little sadness Denise watched her stomach rise and fall, as the water splashed against the floor. A song from another language moved through the vent above her head, and she knew she would never see him again after this night.

In another lifetime this night would have been impossible to accept. But after so much disappointment, Denise made her peace with what she had done. She had seen his results, and had taken the chance to deliver herself into a miracle.

Water flowed underneath the door of the bathroom as Denise dressed to leave. As she walked down the hallway she imagined Damir, stern-faced in the warm water, swimming.

The Blessed Event

I'm gluing pictures of naked people into the photo album I keep under the counter when I get the call. Fish-belly white bodies on vacations away from their kids smush against one another. Each print is a parade of nipples and body hair, pink soles of feet pointing toward a ceiling out of frame, round butts swirling on hotel sheets. It seems impossible that in a world of digital cameras and cell phones there are still people left who use film, but there are. Most are older, and I guess the rest are afraid of their pictures hitting the internet. They're the ones who come to us. Either way, these drugstore customers haven't heard of double-prints, or thought that guys like me might scrapbook them for eternity. They just drop off their disposable cameras or rolls, and wait for me to do what I do.

The call is from my photography professor. He needs me to hold the light kit for a huge wedding up in the Hills tonight. He asks if I have a decent suit, and warns me about professional discretion. I tell him secrecy is not a problem, and finish pasting a bushy housewife onto a page in my album that follows my series of married men getting busy with women who have to be hookers. I'm thinking of putting out a book some day.

That evening I drag the lighting kit up the front lawn of a Spanish style mansion. The drive up is lined with white paper lanterns, and on the lawn two men in tuxedos hold cages filled with doves to be released later. Valets in red jackets and bow ties carefully steer new Bentleys and Mercedes toward a gated parking area. Helicopters from the tabloids circle above, but they're losing the light.

At the front door my professor tests the three cameras around his neck one by one and gives me the rundown. The bride is a big time romance novelist, he says. If I've been to a supermarket magazine isle I've seen her name on the front of at least a dozen paperbacks in thick gold print. This is her eighth wedding. She only marries venture capitalists and ex-cons. If we do a good job we'll catch her next one. He says he's done five of the eight already, and they paid for his summer house in Cabo.

Inside the estate cast members from legal dramas hobnob with networking corporate attorneys and celebrity personal trainers. An assistant to the wedding planner leads us into a back room to set up without even looking up from his iPad.

In the back room the bride's six adopted children smoke cigarettes and watch reruns of *Jersey Shore*. They range in age from twelve to fifteen. The girls are trashy blondes dressed in red slit dresses that show off their bony legs. The boys wear Lakers jerseys, and baseball hats with the stickers still attached like gangsters. They ignore us as we get our gear together.

I spend the night following my professor around with floodlights harnessed to my back. I hold round silver plates out to cast shadows onto the bride who looks like an old Playboy bunny, and onto the groom who belongs on an assembly line. By the time they kiss I'm blind from the bulbs.

In the back room we break everything down. The kids are drinking at the open bar and shouting at each other. A game show host walks by with a nosebleed, and stops to grab two swimsuit models' tits. The professor says I can put this down on my resume after I graduate. No money coming my way he says, but this is good work experience. Then he laughs and talks about buying a boat.

I pocket a roll of film on my way out. I think about all those check-out line magazines dying for the shots, and plan on going to Vegas.

The Man Who Fell Through the Sky

Henry's first wife always said he was simple, and as he sits shirtless on the roof of his garage he can't help but believe she was right. The home they once shared overlooks the biggest amusement park in the Midwest, and as he stares out at the iron spines of roller coasters in the horizon he cradles his belly like a basketball. When he moves one palm up, the fat in his gut settles to the side without a sound. The gym shorts he wears are tighter than they have ever been before, and they gnaw purple lines into his pale doughboy hips. When he moves his other palm up the fat settles heavy in his midsection. Then he lets his belly fall where it will and leans back on his arms, stretching the bubble of himself out toward the sky. It's about to explode.

A structure that was meant to replicate The Eiffel Tower, but instead looks more like a birdcage on stilts, peeps over the tree line which separates his home from the Great Midwest Amusement Park. It looms black in the night while its signal lights shut off one by one. This is the countdown. All the lights on the needle go out before the lights on the observation deck die. For a moment the sky is blank and slate-colored. Rockets wait in cannons. Henry holds his breath, and curls his toes against the roof tiles.

Bombs explode into the air, bursting out in shades of mouthwash green and peppermint reds. Paint-set primary colors streak through the clouds and shower sparks down onto cars hustling out of the Great Midwest parking lot below. Ten minutes pass. Chrysanthemum blossoms are born out in shimmering gold. Streamers howl in great smoke plumes, but Henry can't manage a smile. He can only watch as the chance for cheer passes in the gunpowder clouds.

He used to love the fireworks show when he was married. He would ride his bike down to the river to watch cinders drop into the stream every summer night before Labor Day. He was a young man then. Now that he is middle-aged, divorced, and employed by that same amusement park, the lights don't mean anything at all. On nights like this he makes an effort to feel the way he used to, but the magic never returns.

The last barrage illuminates the downward arches of roller coasters spiraling around the park. The iron arms of new machines made to swing helpless visitors into the stratosphere reflect the firestorm above them. Henry has never allowed himself to be buckled into the park's flying wheels or pinned into its cars. He saw a man's body fly free from The Mangler when he was young, and in his dreams he can still see him floating free in the clouds, howling, never hitting the concrete landscape below. Each time the nightmare plays out he shudders in his sleep, afraid the man's head will split open at his feet at last.

Moving back through his bedroom window carefully, Henry looks over a poem he has been writing for his new wife, who he has never met. Her name is Petunia. She is thirty-two, a single mother of two, and a natural blonde. The picture Henry received from the Ukrainian agency makes her looks silly. Her hair is teased high, her clothes are too tight, and she is wearing so much make-up that she looks like a child who has just discovered lipstick. It's a Glamour Shots kind of picture. Her head is tilted and her hand is pressed thoughtfully to her chin. The poem he is working on only has one line.

Bend me like wire wings

Henry stares at the line in his notebook. He wants to say something about flowers in honor of his wife, or wife-to-be. He isn't sure how these things work in that part of the world. He is only sure that if he doesn't find some tenderness soon he's doomed.

He has written a lot of lies to Petunia to improve his position in her heart. He couldn't resist writing down all the things he wished for himself: that he is younger, better looking, and has never been married. The only comfort he gathers comes from his belief that she must have polished her life story for him as well. She can't be as educated as she says. She must be older. Petunia doesn't sound like Slav name at all. Two thousand dollars into the process now he can't turn back. It is good therapy; a reason to dream. The agency says once the paperwork is finished she could be on a plane any day, but for now he is glad that he has time and afraid of the time he has.

The next morning Henry goes to work at the amusement park in a blue polo shirt with the Great Midwest logo embroidered on the chest. It's covered with grease stains, but his requests for a new one have all been ignored. His manager, who is younger than Henry by twenty years, reminds him that he will have to buy a new shirt if he is unhappy with the one he has. He has stopped asking, and accepted the fact that slobs have no sway.

The roller coasters' steel girders and rails threaten the clouds above the treetops. Their velocities go unchecked. Their trains of chain-driven cars undergo maintenance only once a season at best. There are things Henry knows about Great Midwest that he would never share. He has never told a soul about the person thrown from the The Mangler, or the electrical problems that plagued The Ball Python when it was still in operation. He keeps his distance from the rides that would kill him if they had the chance. Bodies like his weren't made to test the patience of gravity.

Parking by the RV lot affords Henry the only chance for exercise he will get for the next eight hours. It is a good half mile to the park's main gate and the walk gets harder every day. By the time he reaches the gate his armpits have sweated oil slicks under each sleeve. He pushes his key card into the machine to clock in and waddles under the weight of the sun to the booth where he will stand flat-footed until lunchtime. Above him a sign reads "Deep Fried Oreos."

Within the hour, batter is caked on Henry's hands so thick that they become welder's gloves. He can reach into the fryer and pull out a deep fried Oreo without using tongs. When he has the crusted double-stuffed cookie between his clotted fingers, he hands it to the next child in line. The child's mother looks surprised, but not upset. Her face goes into the expression of someone who has just witnessed an unexpected moment of street magic, and Henry imagines that she's decided there are things fat men know about Oreos that the rest of the world will never appreciate.

By lunchtime his relief has come. An acne-scarred teenager with surfer hair pulls up his khaki shorts that fall off his hips, and step behind the cart. Henry has eaten five deep-fried Oreos by this time and has no appetite. He uses his lunch break to toddle around the park and get the blood flowing back into his feet.

He has brought his poem with him, or the one line that constitutes the poem, and in his crusty palms it looks like trash. In his back pocket the paper has steamed to pulp and he understands that this is the life of all true poets, droning through worthless jobs with good lines turning into lint. While his watch marks off the minutes of free time he has remaining, he takes an ink pen out of his pocket and writes down a new line.

Burn me like flower petals

Back at his booth, Henry empties the deep fryers into a rolling metal vat. The oil smells like candy canes soaked in lighter fluid. His polo shirt is heavy with body odor and grease, and the thought of wearing it another day seems as appealing as wearing a dead cat to work. With his shift done, he makes his way to the office to plead his case. If he doesn't get a transfer there is no hope of becoming the man he told Petunia he was. Behind him a young girl pins a new sign to the booth while her friend pours in fresh cooking oil. The sign reads "Deep Fried Snicker Bars."

Inside the park office, Henry's manager is trying to remember the Spanish words for "clean" and "bathroom" so he can get the new maintenance crew members to work. He thinks the word for clean is "levante," and uses "banjo" for bathroom. The confused workers confer with each other and chuckle before walking out the door in search of banjos that need to be lifted. Henry washes the dough from his hands in the water fountain while no one is paying attention and tucks in his shirt. His argument takes shape in his mind.

Henry's supervisor explains that he will have to put a bid in for a transfer. This is the peak season after all, and there aren't many slots left that meet his qualifications. Henry warns that he feels the onset of carpal tunnel syndrome building in his hands, that his arms are showing signs of eczema, and that the worker's-comp settlement could grow larger with each cookie he fries. Finally, his supervisor agrees to transfer him to the water park for the time being, but warns him against false claims. There are penalties to consider, both state and federal.

Henry walks to his car free from the danger of deep fried cookies and sure of the fact that chlorine-resistant bacteria are, at the very least, low-calorie.

There is a letter for Henry when he arrives home. He finds it underneath an advertisement for a real-estate agency that buys homes sight unseen, super-saver coupon fliers, and a brand new credit card ready for activation. He takes his mail with him into the basement of his home and strips before throwing his clothes in the washer. He sits on an unused weight bench as he reads the letter. Promises of romance and soft pleas for patience are neatly typed. The paper work is moving through the proper channels, but more money is needed.

Inside the envelope is a new picture of Petunia. She wears a swimsuit and stands on a shoreline of boulders and stones. She is beautiful, but frowns as if the camera was an intrusion into some private instance in her life. Underneath the picture is a request to electronically transfer another five hundred dollars to the Tatiana Matrimonial Service. The transfer number has changed again.

Henry pays the new matrimonial fee on his latest credit card over the internet. He plans to make his car payment with it as well. He owns his home since his first wife was both successful and eager to be divorced. Because of that the more he spends on credit cards, the more credit cards he gets even. He doesn't think about paying off his cards anymore than he thinks about death. Reality is the worst kind of depression.

In his bedroom he watches television ads for diet pills and home weight sets. He watches hypnotists hawk tapes for weight loss, and dietitians warn about the growing impact to the body brought on by years of poor choices. Fitness is a state of mind, like loving yourself, they all argue. The answer lies within.

Candy-bellied and restless, Henry can't stop thinking. He decides to make a plan. He will write down all the facts as he sees them. This is how daytime talk-show hosts approach life's problems. At his computer he begins to type.

When he finishes listing his woes and ambitions, it strikes him that this is not a plan at all, but a simple history of personal disasters and bad decisions. If he is going to change he has to take action now. He does push-ups on the floor and gets to five, then does sit-ups until he gets to six. It's progress enough for one night.

Back in his bed, Henry sweats as the man is thrown from the roller coaster again and sails through the air, his body closer than he remembers, arms flailing and shadowing the ground. He startles awake then collapses back against the mattress, glad that tomorrow he will be working safely away from the rides, in wading pools filled with screaming children.

The water park of Great Midwest is decorated with concrete alligators bleached by chlorine and the sun. They look like the boulders in Petunia's picture. As he walks into the water park Henry wonders if Petunia would look sad if she straddled them the way kids do for pictures. Plastic parrots are bolted to trees concealing speakers that blare sixties rock songs across the sunburned throng. Middle-aged women sit in deck chairs reading mystery novels that rest on their bellies, while their paunchy husbands toss beach balls back and forth with kids who sport temporary tattoos.

Henry stands in his swim trunks and grins at the white and red parade of bodies that belong behind the wheels of delivery trucks or reception desks. The young ones are tanned and glisten, but the older ones all look the same: pale, frustrated, slumped with guts. He realizes that if a man wants to feel better about his body all he needs to do is visit a water park.

At the water park's office, Henry is assigned a whistle and given a new shirt. The shirt is a tank top that has a picture of a dog riding a surfboard on it. The dog is wearing sunglasses and has its tongue hanging out in the wind. In the mirror Henry studies himself and makes a note to mention to Petunia that he has taken up surfing. He doubts she knows where Ohio is exactly anyway.

His duties at the water park are simple. He is in charge of safety enforcement. This means that he spends most of his day walking from pool to pool, reminding children not to run on the wet pavement and asking people that they not remove the park's floats from the lazy river. When not roaming in search of racing children, he is to keep an eye out for unattended bags that could be snatched up by criminals, and take them to the lost-and-found department on the far side of the park. He counts up the miles he will travel in his mind and feels his stomach contracting already.

By midday the sun is unbearable, and he searches for a spot to rest. His ankles swell as he wanders rows of trees filled with squatters on beach blankets. Towels and coolers have claimed every inch of shade even when their owners are long gone. He worries that he could suffer a heatstroke at any moment, but finds an unattended lifeguard tower overlooking a giant wave pool. The umbrella seems to offers at least a ten degree drop. Once up the tower, he closes his eyes and listens to the sound of water being churned by the wave generators that rumble under him. The waters of the Ukraine must sound nothing like this. He pictures them quiet and solemn, rocky shores broken only by sad-faced women placed there for American dollars. Another line comes to his mind.

I've felt the stones at your feet

Henry's peace mixes with the chlorine lull of the wave pool until he can't keep his eyes open. He dreams of riding a wave that never crests until a stranger strong-arms him awake.

"You're in my seat, chief." The man is muscular though his chest hair has grayed to the color of wood ash.

"Sorry," Henry says, then struggles to move his stiff legs down the ladder. How does he do it? How does that man look so good at his age?

At home that night, Henry adds the line that came to him before he fell asleep by the wave pool to the others he has collected. He knows that three lines don't make a poem, but they might constitute a stanza. A stanza is a good step, and when the lines come together on his computer screen he prints them out and walks around repeating them over and over to himself. He hopes that Petunia speaks English, or at the very least can read English. It is a question he has never asked, and suddenly he is filled with fear that all his heartfelt exaggerations might have been left in the hands of a translator, someone less concerned with the meaning of his letters than he is. He sits down and types an e-mail to the Tatiana Matrimonial Agency demanding to know whether or not Petunia is proficient in English, but doubts it will be answered. They rarely were.

After reciting his stanza to himself until the words break apart into disjointed sounds, Henry turns on the television for company. He watches infomercials where the formerly obese walk around exercise rigs in running shorts. The voice-over announcer talks about getting serious while women pull on weighted cords until their shoulder muscles pop out like chicken cutlets. "Can you believe this woman is a grandmother?" The announcer asks. "This can be you."

Henry wonders if the man at the water park has ever been featured in any of these ads. He wonders if the lifeguard's basement is packed with exercise machines named after jungle cats that feature the signatures of former Mr. Universes. If that's the trick, he vows to use his credit cards to buy whatever the lifeguard suggests. If the older man didn't believe in cable crunches and free weights, he must have found a better way.

Henry does push-ups until he gets to ten, and knocks out his sit-ups until he gets to twelve before heading to bed. Against his pillow, he can hear the rumbling of cars flying free from their tracks. Exhausted, he sleeps so heavy that the man never falls free before he wakes.

Arriving early at the water park the next day, Henry is determined to find the lifeguard. He stacks floats by the lazy river and scans the park for him as the herd moves in. Mothers hurry with children to the deck chairs surrounding the pool so that they can claim the best spot with bath towels before other visitors arrive. Children run to forts fitted with water cannons and sprinklers, and laugh as they blast each other with jets of cold water. Henry wonders if Petunia's children are young enough to laugh at water. He has never asked their ages or anything else about them, and suddenly feels horribly self-centered. Children on boogie boards ride the crests of turbine generated waves. The only lifeguards around to watch them are bored high school kids who stare at their phones and never look up.

The plastic parrot speakers are playing songs by the Beach Boys, Jan and Dean, and The Kinks. They play "Surfing Safari" then follow it up with "Tin Soldier Man," which sounds to Henry like "Tense Older Man," so that's what he sings.

As the afternoon passes Henry has given up on finding the lifeguard and settles down on a bench underneath the picnic shed for lunch. He has a salad. Things in life are like poetry; small actions building towards the whole. His trunks no longer carve welts into his hips.

Just as he finishes the last of his lunch, he sees the lifeguard climbing into the stand by the wave pool. As he lifts himself up onto the stand the muscles harden then settle into his bronze skin. Henry wipes his hands on his surfing dog tank top, and makes his way casually across the wet concrete.

Once Henry gets to the stand where the lifeguard watches children fake drowning one another, he apologizes for sleeping on the job the day before. The lifeguard, whose name is Jerry, tells him not to worry, that he does the same thing most days. Sunglasses, he says, are the key. Mirrored ones are the best, the kind they used to wear on CHiPs.

In the wave pool one child floats face down with his arms spread-eagled. His friends laugh and flail their arms toward the two men standing at the lifeguard stand. Henry starts to take off his sandals and fumbles with his whistle, but Jerry waves him off. The facedown boy looks up at the two and gives them the finger before swimming off with his friends. Jerry says children are fascinated with death because they've never seen it.

Once the drowning game has lost its appeal, children busy themselves with cannonballs and flinging one another off the side of the pool into the waves. Jerry's face draws into a knot and his hands grip the side of the stand until his fingers turn white. Henry asks him how he stays in such good shape at his age, but Jerry doesn't answer him. Instead he rips off his sunglasses, and marches on shaking legs to the end of the pool where he yells at the boys in front of their startled mothers. Henry can only make out the word "concussion" over the sound of splashing and giggles. When Jerry comes back he fishes a plastic two liter out of his bag. Henry asks how he gets away with drinking that much soda to make small talk. Jerry holds up the bottle, and says it's mostly vodka.

While Jerry drinks, Henry talks about trying to cut weight. He asks Jerry what he does, but gets brushed off again. Jerry has never worked out a day in his life.

"You're lucky that you don't have to work out. I've got these bad genes," Henry says. "My ex-wife said I must have been one of those fat babies that stays both, whatever that means."

"Genes got nothing to do with it," Jerry says. "I used to weigh a hundred pounds more than I do now before I took this stinking job."

"I don't get it," Henry says. "I mean, you just sit all day."

Jerry takes another drink and nods, "That's true. That's what's so bad about it. I have to watch them try to bust their heads all day long."

According to Jerry, his secret for staying fit is pure unadulterated fear. He was hired to be a lifeguard since he used to be a commercial diver. What the park didn't know was that he stopped diving because he almost drowned in a water tower and never got his nerves back. Now the idea of swimming cements the joints in his knees and elbows to the point he can hardly stand it. Each day he sits down and contemplates someone's son or daughter drowning at his feet. It fills him with so much terror that his body sheds pounds faster than he can buy new clothes. Children launch themselves headfirst into the waves, and his heart rate doubles. He tells Henry that every day he works he wants to quit before something terrible happens, but the thought of becoming a broke slouch again keeps him from giving up. "Fear keeps you fit," Jerry says. "It's natural. There are no big guys on death row."

Henry doesn't argue. He longs to make Petunia fawn over him when they meet, and decides to terrify himself into a dreamboat.

Fear for you has made me

The line starts a new stanza, and Henry takes his poem out of the glove box to scrawl it down. The roller coasters shake in high winds as he drives off towards home.

Romance for Delinquents

On the roof of his garage, Henry watches the fireworks coming from the park. He imagines Petunia sitting next to him on a blanket with her children. They watch the sparks splinter overhead and he promises to take them swimming every day he works. He longs for them. He has spent his entire life on the outskirts of a celebration, and it seems a poverty to him that he hasn't shared all that joy.

The Mangler was once the largest wooden roller coaster in the United States. It was one of the last mega-coasters built before steel tubes replaced solid oak frames bolted into concrete pillars. There are no tricks to The Mangler. It doesn't spiral in loops or invite its riders to enjoy the novelty of riding while standing up or with their feet dangling free. It just offers a series of drops so profound that people with heart conditions, those who are or might be pregnant, or have any history of back problems are forbidden to ride it. The gravitational force the ride produces is equivalent to those an astronaut faces upon re-entry. Though it has taken lives in the past, two over the last decade, and been the cause of several personal injury lawsuits, it remains in operation at Great Midwest since it's still the park's biggest draw. The line to ride it is over three hours long on most days. At the tail end of the line today Henry waits in a cold sweat.

Coming to the Great Midwest on his day off is a first for Henry. He has eaten enough deep-fried, over-cheesed, batter-dipped, jumbo-sized food in his life that he has removed the mirror in his bathroom so that he never has to see his body. The park is incredibly crowded in the summer, and it gives him that awful shopping-mall-at-Christmas-time feeling that makes him keep his distance when he can. This day is different, and no crowd could stop him no matter how far away he has to park. He has come with a purpose—transformation.

The line for The Mangler reminds him of the deep-fried Oreo stand where he used to work. The air is greasy and smells like armpits. People sweat all around him in the maze of rails that lead visitors up to the platform where the cars depart. For almost an hour he takes baby steps forward, careful not to let his stomach graze the people in line ahead of him or to touch the rails which have guided millions of dirty hands up towards the machine.

In high school Henry was a member of the Future Farmers of America. At home in his basement he still has the blue corduroy jacket with his name and state embroidered on the back, although the owl and plow patch on the front is missing. While a member of the club, Henry had to watch educational films about what happens to cattle at a slaughterhouse and the images comes back to him now. Tired-eyed beasts take measured steps. Their bodies brush against the rails of the processing plant. They move upwards, always upwards, and never know what's waiting at the top. His mouth goes dry.

He has cleared the first maze and made it up a flight of stairs to the second. Like the coaster, the maze of rails and stairs is made of solid oak. People have carved their names in the posts over the years and encircled them with hearts. There are ink pen markings that look like skulls and flowers, and phone numbers long since disconnected are dug into the wood. He looks for poetry to steal. He hopes that someone else only had one good line in them and wrote it on the rails in case someone else could make it into a real poem, but nothing stands out.

There is a sound like a storm brewing above him. Beams of light snake down between the planks overhead as the grinding of iron and clatter of chains get louder. Suddenly a bomb blast of screams goes off as The Mangler sends thirty people in fifteen cars towards the ground at speeds their bodies would never face walking the Earth. The sound leaves him dumb. He is simply moving with the herd. He can't see the roller coaster. He is inside the factory. His high school teacher told his FFA class that the cows never see the hooks and knives ahead of them, and now he believes him. He can only see backs and heads, penned in, moving toward the sky.

After two and a half hours of waiting, he is too weak to walk. His blood moves through his veins like buttermilk. He can see the cars now. Young children and couples step into them. The roller coaster operators are distracted kids who fumble with their phones as they take charge of everyone's lives. He knows they never check the chains. He knows they show up late and mark off their safety checklists without looking over anything. He knows all this without asking. They haven't learned about death either.

A young girl in a blue Great Midwest polo shirt motions him into a car at the end of the roller coaster while her friend walks down the line of cars absently tugging on the safety bars. Henry wants to tell the girl that he can't ride. He wants to tell her about the man who fell through the sky and never landed, but she's already gone. He can see her raise a thumb to her friend who's back at the controls. The chains jerk to attention, and the cars rush off before Henry can say a word.

His mind feels like a beehive as he watches Great Midwest spread out beneath him. He can't answer simple questions now. He can't remember his name or what he had for lunch. He can only watch the sky grow before him and hear the sound of chains dragging underneath his seat. They pop like bones breaking. At the top of the first huge drop, he searches the horizon. He sees the rest of the amusement park and the stream by his home. He sees the wave pools and the food stands. He sees the whole map of his life before The Mangler sends him to the ground.

Henry is weightless. He is perfectly clear in mind and spirit for a split second before his body feels like it's ripped from an airplane at altitude.

The world disappears. Everything around him moves forward and backward at the same time. Night and day pass and return every second. He falls through the sky for two minutes, but never lands. He is safe now. The chains have brought him back to the living. When the girl lifts his safety bar, he tries to speak but has no language. None exist.

There are times when people are blessed with the ability to step outside their bodies for fleeting moments and take in the beauty and disaster of their lives. Some people have this ability all the time. They are given titles like shaman, guru, or mystics. For most people this chance only comes once. It happens during car crashes, in the middle of war, during open-heart surgery, in drug overdoses and births. Henry fell through the sky.

Henry walks to the main office of Great Midwest and quits his job. Then he goes home where he informs the Tatiana Matrimonial Agency via e-mail that he will be arriving within the week to pick up his wife and children whether the paperwork is finished or not. He books plane tickets online, one to Kiev, four back to the United States. He takes a flier from his desk and within an hour sells his home for a tenth of its value. He takes a shower and thinks about the days to come when he will live in a cramped apartment with bad credit. He dreams of promising a summer trip to Great Midwest to his new family who will be thrilled at the prospect of concrete alligators and gravy smothered French fries.

Henry no longer believes in steps, only blind dives into the unknown.

A Long Line of Liars

My Grandpa Jake worked the overnight shift at a gospel station outside of Wichita where hyped up on Benzedrine five nights a week, he broadcast sermons across the plains that proclaimed angels walking among men. While the records played he made time with every farm girl he could coax into visiting the station for his special late night tour. He was out of high school and had the world by the skirt until the reverent folks at the draft board took notice of his program, and decided they needed him for the war effort. They drug him in, and told him that he was going to be a radio man for the U.S. Navy. Nine girls who'd never met each other wrote letters to the board begging that they reconsider taking him away. Each of them tearfully explained that they were engaged to be married to my Grandpa

Jake, and broken up at the prospect of losing their one true love. Even though there wasn't a lie in one of those letters he was shipped off to sea in no time flat if only to save more gentle hearts like theirs.

The Second World War was picking up steam back then, and my Grandpa Jake wasn't about to be a hero if he could help it. He learned soon enough that being a radio man for the Navy had nothing to do with playing records and keeping the microphone turned off so that no old farmer heard his daughter panting in delight. The Navy wanted radio men for bombers which gave handsome young men like him thin odds of coming home, so he transferred with forged papers and became the newest ship's photographer on a monolith of an aircraft carrier headed for the sunny shores of Waikiki.

As a ship's photographer, my Grandpa Jake passed his time with pineapple juice and cigarettes while enjoying the rolling lull of ocean beneath his feet. The only break in his vacation came on Tuesdays, which were meant for ship's maintenance regardless of one's charge. To solve the problem of sincere labor, he stole a monkey wrench and twenty feet of rope that he kept hidden in his foot locker. When every Tuesday rolled around he carried his wrench and rope up one deck and down the other from morning to night. He'd say "Have to go to deck three" to the officers who stopped him, or "Ordered to deck nine" if his friends asked for a hand. Then in his rack at night he read magazines articles about how to strike it rich.

My Grandpa Jake went AWOL when his carrier finally came to rest on the shores of Hawaii, and spent long nights flirting with all the Tiki girls in the local bars. They made a living off the Navy boys, but they had the best of intentions since charity comes in all forms. He met my Grandma Pearl one night when the MPs were rounding up stragglers. She had a room above the bar for lost souls like my Grandpa Jake, as angels often do.

After enough time had passed the Navy gave up on finding him, and my Grandpa Jake and Grandma Pearl set up shop out back of a bar away from the base with camera gear he'd stolen from the ship. It wasn't a sin since his tax dollars paid for that camera as much as they paid for the bombs his former employer seemed set on using to blow up the world. It was a grace he had coming to him for leaving so many girls unmarried at home.

Once they got set up, my Grandpa Jake grew his beard out and took to wearing loud flowery shirts. Grandma Pearl got a hula skirt, and finally found coconuts big enough to make into bra. The Tiki girls helped them get the word out to the Navy boys, and together my grandparents fleeced young men from flat lands who were desperate to have a picture of themselves with their arms wrapped around a real hula girl to show the boys back home. That was the first step of their plan.

The next step was to take the money they made, and buy a modest home in a respectable neighborhood, preferably one filled with young Navy wives who were mothers and devout Bible believers. Once they had the house, my Grandma Pearl would get to socializing and tell all those sweet mothers about her room over the bar with details that would beat any picture. The thought that a woman as kind to strangers as my Grandma Pearl lived on their very street would worry those fine young women until they forced their respectable husbands to buy the house from my Grandpa Jake for more than twice what he paid. He'd strike a hard bargain and defend his wife's honor till there was enough money to let their dream house go no matter how bad he hated to. Then they'd move three streets over, and do it again. Their cycle had a way of repeating itself until the hatred in the world died down, but they learned that faith in the Lord and real estate were sound investment.

Once they got back to the states, my grandparents bought up eighty acres of land, and became millionaires by selling real estate courses through the mail. They had seven exceptional children who went on to preach the Gospel in baseball stadiums, and open a nationwide chain of subdivisions that were tailored to faithful families in the market for a moral place to raise their children. My grandparents retired to a resort they built where former Tiki girls and aging G.I.s could be friendly with one another, and never worry about what the world thought or knew. Now the rest of my family is living high and spreading the good word. This leaves only me to tell the truth.

Sea Change

Remi sits with his back against the wall and turns little sea shells into arrowheads with a steel file, the same one he uses to make conk shells into knives. Outside on the beach, broken glass catches the moon. Sand lifts up from the carpet and grits between his toes. Every breath he takes tastes like salt. This is the beginning. He knows what he has to do. There's a pistol on the bed. He bought it out of the trunk of a Lincoln at the Seaside Flea Market on Ocean Boulevard weeks ago. He puts down the file and closes his eyes. The sea is in his head. The tourists are coming. The baby names are waiting. No relief is in sight.

On the night stand he lifts the phone's receiver to his ear and lets its drone roll over him. She found her way back to him again. He tosses the receiver to the side and goes back to work.

He switches on the shark fin lamp by the bed, and knocks over the ring box he's carried around so long that most of its velvet is worn ragged. There are restraining orders next to the wall behind the night stand. If he could explain himself he would tell you that this isn't how it started. He'd tell you that you've caught him at a bad time—in between. There are envelopes packed with songs by his keyboard. The ocean has a heart too. He would explain that it started with her, and that he can't catch up.

Remi rests himself onto the bed as his fingers find the keys. Some men lose themselves on purpose. Losing makes you lighter.

BBCD

BBCD

BBCE

BBCE

The Sanyo keyboard on his lap runs on D batteries and is covered with Christmas stickers. Remi wrote his name on the back of it with a silver marker when he got it. He was just a kid then singing "Let the Sun Shine In." The keyboard was the first Christmas present he ever played with more than two weeks. He's saved it from garage sales and it saved him when his life turned to tar. When it was new it came with a pop rock song book and stickers. He had to carefully glue a sticker onto each key like the diagram in the instruction book. In his room he presses down the B, C, and D in rhythm, playing from page one of the songbook. The electronic notes of "I Just Called to Say

I Love You" fill him up. The telephone stays off the hook.

The stickers on the keys are impossible to read now. Some are rubbed out and grimy, some are missing all together, and most look like dried up spit wads underneath some high school kid's desk. Remi knows where the missing ones belong. He can see them underneath his eyelids. The first bars come easy. A man shouldn't forget things he loves.

The mother voice in Remi's head sings, "Tina is a special name for a special girl like you. Tina is a sunny day that won't let your heart be blue."

Then the mother voice falls away and the lullaby is axed. What difference does it make? The mother voice is a focusing technique he was trained to use when writing songs for the company. It's cheap and silly. He feels like a motivational speaker. He pushes the keyboard off his lap and listens to the dial tone. He knows this will be the last song he will ever write. He's earned it.

He puts the receiver back on the telephone, and moves his tape recorder onto the bed. The spools of tape rewind until a light turns orange and the microphone labeled button flashes.

Remi's uncle owns the seaside rental. He lets him to stay here to do his work when the honeymoon season has passed. His uncle considers it a charitable sponsorship of the arts and writes the expense off on his tax returns. Remi has told his uncle that he is composing a symphony, and his uncle likes the idea as much as Remi does. It doesn't matter what the truth is since the idea of a symphony is easier to sell. It's easier to understand than freelance children's songwriter. Remi doesn't believe symphonies exist anymore.

Last autumn Remi took the songwriting job. He found it advertised in the back of a local free newspaper. The company sent him a list of two-hundred common children's names. It was all easy enough before her. All he had to do was match each name on the list with an original three-minute-long song that was appropriate for children. No sex, drugs, or swearing. No God or politics. Keep them clean and neutral. He just had to write songs about how wonderful Johnny was, or what a pretty girl Ellie is. The company warned him about complicated arrangements and words too big for children to understand. They wanted sing-song happy tunes for vacationing parents. For the last year Remi has written songs dripping with sunshine and rainbows, and forwarded them to a corporate office.

"Tina" is spelled out in big black letters on the cover of a notebook next to his pillow. He has saved her for last. She is always there at the end because she was the beginning.

The company Remi works for owns factories in Mexico City where hundreds of children the same age as its consumers glue plastic mermaids to fiberglass seashells all day long. They own screen-printing operations in Chihuahua that work around the clock stamping out T-shirts that read "Sun Your Buns in Daytona" or "One Tequila, Two Tequila, Three Tequila, Floor." The company has cornered the market on tourist trap impulse buys including the songs Remi writes, which they refer to as "personalized musical mementos." Music and lyrics equal plastic sunglasses and a sandal keychain.

Romance for Delinquents

Everything in the room suddenly seems out of order, and Remi stretches his arms to the ceiling to remind himself that he is not the carpet or the phone. He has to take stock to center himself: his toy keyboard, a professional keyboard covered with plastic, the notebook, the envelopes, and the outdated tape recorder in its case. Above his bed there is a picture of his uncle's ex-wife leaning against a palm tree. It must have been taken a decade before their divorce. She's all smiles and tits in the sun. He wonders if his uncle knows she's still here. His arms fall to his sides as he steps over a stack of love letters that belong in the trash.

Books pile up in the bathroom sink. The soggy cover of one promises to tell its readers how to name their child by their star sign. Paperbacks on the back of the toilet cover Scottish names, Indian names, Jewish names, Catholic names. All the babies in the world are waiting for a word to call themselves.

Not everything in the room has to do with work. It's a keepsake junkyard. There are sweatshirts he can't throw away in the dresser. Programs from piano recitals line the medicine cabinet. He puts yellow paper love letters back in a shoebox after tying them with a hair ribbon that's only threads now. He slides the gun away in a drawer.

Months ago the world was brighter. His songs were coming along as fast as plastic mermaids on a conveyor belt. Some nights he would write ten before walking to a FedEx box where they would be spirited away in the bottom of overnight planes. That time, when the keyboard played and the melody didn't matter, is washing away.

Remi pulls a shirt over his head in the kitchen and walks toward the stairs. He looks in the empty bedrooms and wonders how many people were made in them. He puts his hands against his stomach, and he knows that something inside is slowly unwinding.

The rentals are mostly abandoned this time of year. Three white cars have been stranded on the street. Weeds have climbed up the pine stilts meant to save the house from the surf. There is no one to welcome. No visitors to impress. In February the honeymooners are still huddled up in Indiana or Minnesota, or wherever else they migrate from. Remi is the last man on Earth. It is a relief, a moment past music.

When Remi reaches the back deck he feels a fever paint across his face. His legs give a little as he sees himself walking on the surface of the moon. The sad facts of his life add up in the after all. Music majors get silly jobs. They serve secretaries lunch at kitschy restaurants, or are filed away to write jingles for breakfast cereals and Chevrolets.

The radio outside is on. The weather report of tropical storms mumbles to itself, but doesn't bother him with hurricane gossip. He locks the door as he leaves, as he has every night since September, and thinks about the ring waiting for him in the room. After Tina's song he can disappear. The ring is just another worthless souvenir.

Outside the wind carries the scent of dried leaves as it elbows its way between empty hotel towers. South Carolina winters are like that. Remi sits on a wooden bridge and feels the cool rush of air pull at his sleeve. This is what happens when summer dies. On the beach the world exhales all winter long, following the past and ever onward to the people who stay away when the sun is gone. Sitting on the bridge he knows that at this moment no one can touch him. Redemption is a flash, a big bright light that remains in the distance.

He walks away from the bridge when the wind dies away, and makes his way through the sand until he reaches the sidewalk. The ocean is a black forever polishing rocks.

The water will take lives when the sun and tourists return in the summer. It's meant to. There's no need to blame the old villains—sharks and rip tides. The water is enough. Tourists will fall asleep on floats in the surf and be pulled out to sea by the current. The shore will disappear, and they'll be gone forever because they didn't open their eyes in time. For a moment it seems too much to take, the stark inevitable, but he gets himself right and marches down the sidewalk.

Along the beach block after block of closed hotels sit locked in the geometry of empty swimming pools and parking lots. Next to them are the storefronts where Remi's songs will be sold to vacationers. Smiling parents will buy them while old women twist their little girls' hair into stringy rows of braids. Later they will abandon them in the closets of guest rooms or in cardboard boxes buried in garages.

Down the street Sam's Diner is open twenty-four hours. It is the kind of place no one plans to go to, they just end up there. Inside the diner one long linoleum countertop runs the length of the restaurant separating the paying customers from line cooks with criminal records. At the counter every level of society eats shrimp burgers and fried clams shoulder to shoulder democratically.

As Remi sits on a cracked red leather stool a melody moves down his arms toward his fingers. He orders a coffee and nervously pours one packet of sweetener after another into it until it's like drinking through sugarcane.

Tina's song has to be special, not another fluffy singsong piece he's written in the past. The words to "The Sun Doesn't Shine without Austin," and "Bedtime for Bethany" return to embarrass him. He struggles to forget all the dumb tunes he's hacked out as his fingers tap the countertop, off-beat and awkward as first love. When he can, he leaves.

Walking back toward the condo he accepts the fact that the rest of his family is smarter than he is. No other member of his family ever bothered to learn an instrument or sing outside of a church choir. They each have an ordinary job. They work in education, engineering, or defense contracting. Some, like his uncle, own businesses successful enough to take for granted. His family members have 401(k)s and fantasy football teams. He knows that at different times they are the same as the people who come to the beach to forget about their day jobs and get sunburned in deck chairs or walk through outlet malls. The other members of his family can tell anyone on the street what they do for a living in five words or less. They can let go.

When people ask Remi what he does for a living his face twists no matter how hard he tries to fight it.

"Have you ever seen those kiosks at the beach that sell sunglasses and postcards?" he will ask the interested party. Most times they'll nod and try to look interested.

"Have you ever seen the ones where you can buy a song with

your child's name in it?" They frown, laugh, or look back. Other times they just shake their heads no.

"That's what I do. I write those songs." The people will laugh in amazement, or simply smile politely. Then they leave him feeling naked and ridiculous.

To beat them, he's started to make up stories when the questions come. The cashier with four leaf clover tattoo on her face at Sam's believes he was fired from Broadway for drinking too much. She has invited him to AA meetings, and offered to say a prayer with him on more than one occasion. His uncle believes he will be the next Mozart, though he has no idea who Mozart is other than a name. His parents believe he is getting better now, and that the medicine he said he takes is helping. It is easier to like the person they see in him, the one full of promise.

The vaguely curious never want to know more about what he does for a living, so they never learn the truly worst part of it. When you write songs for names, you have to write happy tunes for names that hurt you.

When people name their children they face two dilemmas. First, most of the names they like are taken. They belong to cousins, celebrity babies, some other newborn or the kid down the street. The second problem is that a lot of names have already become stained by their past lives. You can't name your child Jason if some kid named Jason picked on you in grade school. Names are little scars, and everyone has some name that is soured in the back of their psyches. Tina is Remi's scar. First loves always have the worst names.

Wandering from the sidewalk and up a flight of split oak stairs toward the fishing pier, he thinks about Tina. Not the Tina he loved, but the name itself— joined syllables that are only sounds in the air. Tina is one of those names, trailer park like Crystal, or even worse, Krystal with a K. Tina is a bad blonde dye job with creeping roots. It's almost as bad as Candy, or any name that is joined with the middle name Jo, Jean or Lynn. If he could explain himself he would let you know that he doesn't believe all Tinas in the world are ruined. Only that the ratio is skewed toward the negative.

But for now there is only the name creaking from the boards under his feet. The sound of it scratches the inside of his ear canals leaving tiny claw marks on his anvil, his horseshoe, the drum of his inner ear next to his mind. Staring through the boards he can see the waves beating beneath him. Silver-bodied sand sharks dart underneath the surface searching for scraps of bait. Sand crabs carry shiny chewing gum wrappers down beneath the water to places only they can go. They are biding their time.

As he follows the concrete path back to the condo, the weight of galaxies presses down on him from above. The motion of stars threatens him, makes him run for cover. He races toward an ending.

In his room a book covering classical Greek names falls from the bed. Remi pulls the notebook to him and finds only bad beginnings without ends. Things are how they should be. With an ink pen in hand he struggles to focus. "Tina is a special name/ For a special girl like you/ Tina is a sunny day/ That won't let your heart be blue."

The lyrics lie, and welts of blue ink cover the lyrics in slick tornadoes before the inspiration leaves him. At the window he tries to imagine the other side of the world, what people are doing there at this very minute, but instead the home movie plays in his head.

His window is a screen. The home movie in his head has no soundtrack: two high school kids in love, the oldest mistake, fear, a clinic in the next town, her going away, his resenting her, threats and the nowhere. The movie is an awkward echo that has followed him to this minute. His hands cover the box. He wanted to do right. He trusted her. He couldn't forgive her taking so much, years ago marching toward this moment, and all his nights spent walking. The movie cuts out right after he mourns the half him she ended before it had a name.

He picks up the phone, and knows she is happy. She has learned to let go.

He pulls love letters stained with perfume from underneath his mattress. The letters she wrote are stacked under the letters he wrote, but never sent. After she fell away, she had told him that she loved him with a part of herself that he couldn't love back, so he wrote her letters she could never read. It was an answer then, but he couldn't stop. He knows that he has spent too many years writing things she will never read.

Tina's most recent phone number is on the night stand. She's getting harder to reach, but regardless of what the courts say this night is for her.

The pages of his notebook are running out. Bad starts litter the floor. "Tina is a special name/ For a special girl like you." Some day this song will be wrapped in cellophane on a rack next to someone airbrushing hearts onto a license plate. His eyes are open. The words in front of him don't matter anymore than a puka shell bracelet. His work three months from now will have all the significance of a shark tooth necklace. "Tina is the terrible name/That your mom gave to you/ Tina was the heartless bitch/ Who broke my heart in two." The mother voice inside him has no remorse. "Tina was an evil girl/That laughed when I cried/ Tina won't return my calls/ She never loved, just lied." The orange light from the tape recorder flashes. The wheels turn the tape.

Remi seals the master tape in an envelope, and stacks it with the others. As he walks down the hall his fever returns. Tomorrow morning this song will be flown away with all the others. Inside his chest there is a new slack. His ears ring like feedback from a busted transistor.

Lying on the beach, he thinks about what is ahead of him while the sun is off warming the other side of the world. He knows there is a grand connection between everything in existence. One thing leads to another. Hands touch hands. Some let go. Some don't. He goes back to his room to finish.

Love letters cover the bed. The gun sits by the phone. He breathes in the rolling black endless outside his room. The television across from the bed scatters loud static like a chant. This is the sound of the undertow, and its covers him.

Every love letter is read and torn in two. He's reached the crescendo. He cocks the hammer of the pistol back as he dials the phone. His ears are on the crashing, the breaking, the static, the hum. The toy keyboard waits in his lap.

"Hello," her voice says after a pause, drowsy, far away.

Remi wraps the phone cord around his arm and pulls it tight. "Tina. This is for you." It ends like this.

BBCD

BBCD

BBCE

BBCE

Click.

The gun fires into the telephone, and shatters the plastic receiver and night stand. Smoke fills the room as he staggers to the wall and rips the cord out before he collapses back onto the bed. It is the last she will hear of him. The gun smokes on the floor. Now she has something to think about when time rolls slow, and her own questions that will never be answered.

When he can stand, he walks to a construction dumpster to pile in memories. Love letters fall onto drywall dust as the gun vanishes between scraps of wood. The ring he keeps to let go. He knows where it belongs.

As he wades into the surf he feels his feet bury and unbury themselves in the sand. The sea change is coming. The tide rolls out as he reaches back and throws. The ring flies through the air against the field of stars until it drowns in the waves. He trudges out from the wash while sand crabs skitter from beneath the foam. They hurry to drag the ring down into places only they can reach.

The tide brushes the back of his legs as he leaves the water. Soon the sun will come back, and he will be new again. He wants you to know this is the beginning.

The Problem With Pretty Girls

They pick you up with an open bottle of vodka wedged between their seat belt and the emergency brake. They hold a lit joint between their fingers while they talk to your dad in the driveway. Their car has never had an oil change. Its tags are expired. Before you make it two blocks they race past a parked police car with the stereo blaring. Their arms are in the air, hands off the wheel and pressed against the ceiling. They're laughing already. Nothing can touch them. They wonder why you're so scared?

The Physics of Love

Skip through your radio dial and miss every station. Focus on what is impossible to make out, a station garbled by power lines. The DJs should be a mystery. If you can distinguish a diet soda ad from a pop music single you are still too close. You only want static. Why? Because that static scratching through the speakers is electrical interference, and a very small portion of that is composed of microwaves. Those microwaves began as photons eons ago, and were born in the instance of the Big Bang. That static contains the echo of everything that ever has and ever will exist being created. Everything hurtles random through space, but no one thing and no one person remains lost.

Andy sat alone in the recliner that used to belong to his father the genius. Down in the basement he factored numbers out loud, the powers and digits muffled by concrete walls and cardboard boxes filled with outdated textbooks. Under the house he was sure to be left alone, so he stayed underground since being left to his own devices was all he ever wanted. The wood above his head creaked as his mother paced in the kitchen. He could hear each chair squeak, every cough. She had to haunt him again even though she had moved into an apartment complex for active seniors years ago when her divorce was final. Andy concentrated on the numbers in his head, and tried to bury thoughts of her with higher math. He switched on the radio on his lap when he began to type. The keystrokes above his head nailed into him, and he knew he'd find no relief until that cherry voice came to him again.

The broken down recliner was a reminder of his father that his mother hadn't been able to throw out. It had survived when awards, honorary doctorates, and storage bins filled with theoretical mathematical journals had all found their way to the shredder or the dump. Had the recliner been less of an unmanageable wreck it would have been carried up from the basement years ago, destined for the Sisters of Mercy, but it was solid oak underneath. Neither he nor his mother could remember how it ever got down in the basement in the first place, but like the bulky boxes of outdated textbooks it was there to stay.

Only the recliner, the textbooks, and the carefully organized stacks of lecture notes the college had sent over reminded Andy that he had a father at all. He read through the notes in order to watch his father stray from the path of reasonable scientific endeavors into the current valley of pop culture physics he wallowed in. His course titles told the story: Introduction to Quantum Theory, Intermediate Physics, Beginning Quantum Mathematics, Physics and Game Theory, The Physics of Love, etc. Love had ruined his father's progress. There should have been enough beauty in the 43,000 galaxies of the near universe, in the unfathomable weight of it all, to keep him satisfied. Instead he'd become a talking head, and spent more time on NPR than in the lab. These were second-hand observations. Andy knew it. He hadn't spoken to his father in years so his hypothesis about his life's trajectory could be completely flawed. It didn't matter now. The show was about to begin.

The radio station broadcast the local weather forecast as he tongued the inside of his cheek. Its call letters played out on a xylophone as his fingers traced the ancient cigar burns left in the chair by his father's Dutch Masters. The voice of a young boy filled the basement, "This is Cherokee East Radio!" Inhaling, he pressed his back into the cushions which still smelled like the Pine-Sol his mother coated them with to kill off the scent of the man who left her for better times.

One shoe fell to the floor, followed by the other. The sharp pain behind his eyes dulled. The clock on the wall read 2:15. It was Thursday afternoon; Angel's time to shine. Above him his mother sat at the dinner table and typed out angry single-spaced letters against the proposed construction of a local casino. Angel's voice came to him over the airwaves in sophomoric tones to cover the clicking metal beat of his mother's outrage.

"Um, hello everyone out there! I'm Angel, and I'm a sophomore here at Cherokee East High. You're listening to the voice of Cherokee radio! Go Tribe!"

It was standard procedure. Every student DJ started their show with their name and class, which reminded him of reruns of *The Mickey Mouse Club* he watched as a child. For a moment he wondered what Angel might look like in a tight Annette Funicello sweater and one of those mouse ear beanies, but no picture developed. Today he decided she had red hair and an arch of freckles that ran across the middle of her face.

"I hope everyone is having a great day today! I'm going to play some awesome music for you all the way up to the three o'clock hour." She sounded like a real DJ already, and he wondered how old she was. Fifteen? Sixteen? He was thirty-five so it didn't make a difference. He knew what he felt, and admired her from a distance.

"Okay, um, first up we have an oldie but goodie from Pavement." It took her a second to find her place. He could tell by the way she stammered that she was shy. It was charming. When she said "Pavement" she popped the P. It was a bad habit for the airwaves, but there was something seductive to it; lips popping to make the sound.

For the next half-hour he listened to the records Angel played, and searched for clues. What did these songs mean to her? How tall is she? Had she even kissed a boy? Is she one of those girls who play with their hair during calculus? There were riddles hidden in song lyrics and the things she said.

Too soon the show ended. In the kitchen the typewriter keys clacked away, and his headache returned. His mother ranted on the paper with sweat beading underneath her perm. It would be hours before she left for cocktails and poker games with friends. He decided to wait her out. He didn't want to talk to her. He only wanted to think about Angel, and get ready for the lottery board.

You have to understand that the algebraic axiomatization of probability theory proposes the idea of random variables. Wild cards if you will. Probability distributions are based on the expectation of each random variable. If the variables are unknown, and cannot therefore be expected, everything becomes equal. Anything can happen, and no one thing is anymore unlikely than the next. Now, Bayesians would argue that an event's probability is based on how often a single event occurs. But in the universe, one could conversely argue that everything is occurring at some place in time, even the least likely things. The House doesn't always win.

Andy drove to his job at the lottery board while listening to the tapes he'd made of Angel's past shows. The drive was long enough that he could listen to one complete show and the start of another before being interrupted by the outside world. If he focused his eyes into the distance of power lines and strip malls it was like she was riding next to him, reminding him about prom-committee meetings and talking about free summer concerts. Who was taking her to the prom? She hadn't said. Would she sleep with him?

Once his car reached the bleached mustard lines of the state lottery commission's parking lot her voice cut out. He swallowed the last of his morning coffee, and tried to calm down. He was too stiff for the door.

The lottery commission was a good job for Andy. He worked in the claimant department so most days he was left alone to read the textbooks he brought from home or work on his equations. His father had left him with two things before he bolted with a research assistant: the ability to lose himself in the abstract world of theoretical physics, and a complete inability to interact with people he thought less of casually.

Most of the day he sat hunched over his desk trying to work out knots of logic and conjecture that traveled from one page to the next. He was hopeful. Einstein had started off as a patent clerk stamping tickets. Stephen Hawking had said he was wrong about most things. Everything seemed up for grabs and out of reach at the same time. All he needed was a discovery, one sound universal law of randomization or a new way of thinking about time. Then he would be rewarded. He would be famous enough to have a home his mother couldn't drop in on anytime she liked, and rich enough to leave cubicle land behind.

His fellow staffers at the lottery commission didn't bother to talk to him unless their numbers didn't add up. For the most part they just kept their distance the way people do when their desks are too close together. Only his supervisor, Marsha, tried to make nice.

Marsha was a pathetic mascot for the lottery commission in his eyes, a grandmother face for gambling. She had her picture by the door in a gold frame, a token for all her years of service. Every time a big winner stepped forward to collect their winnings she was the one who passed the over-sized check to them in front of the television cameras. She had seen so many career losers strike it rich that she believed that anyone, even on the worst day of their life, could be rescued. This conviction wouldn't allow her to watch him sulk. She told him that she planned to reaffirm his belief in the possibility of happiness, to which he asked that she not bother.

Marsha's first effort to awaken Andy's belief in salvation was to make him catalogue all the state lottery winners from the mid-eighties to present by age and amount won. She hoped this would illustrate the fact that anyone from a teenager to a pensioner had stumbled into fortune by no means grander than the purchase of a dollar ticket. He coolly turned in the report a few days past his deadline. Listing numbers alone had done nothing to persuade him that random miracles occur in part because he couldn't see the people behind the figures and appreciate the impact of their newfound deliverance.

After the report, Andy started finding random newspaper articles on his desk when he returned from his lunch hour. They were warm human-interest stories. One was about a pair of newlyweds who struck in rich when they found old movie posters hidden behind the walls of their first home while renovating. Another was about a woman who went to her local Target every Saturday and browsed through the baby registry to buy gifts for strangers simply because she loved children. She would spend hundreds of dollars a month on gifts that were shipped anonymously to people she would never meet. It had been Marsha's hope that these stories would make him smile, but they only confused him and ended up in the trash. It seemed he had no human interest at all.

Lastly, lottery tickets started appearing in his workspace. They were hidden inside the stacks of lecture notes on his desk or wedged in his claimant files. Employees of the commission weren't supposed to play the lottery, but it was Marsha's hope that if he could just hit one ticket then he would understand her point of view. Better yet, if the prize was big enough, he could go off and find whatever would make him happy and the rain cloud would be lifted from the office. Her efforts were in vain. Like the news articles before them, all the tickets found their way into a trash can lined with dead ideas.

The workday wound down, and there were no winners to bother with. Andy drove home listening to Angel's show from last Thursday with a thought growing in the back of his mind he hadn't been able to shake. He had never written fan mail in his life, but sometimes the most profound effects, such as atomic blasts, begin with the smallest of things: a single atom torn apart, neutrons spinning free, Dear Angel.

The first line took eight drafts alone. Pouring over a legal pad, Andy considered his options. If he came off too old it might give her the creeps, or she might laugh about it with friends. If he came off too young it might sound fake, and she would think his letter was a dumb prank. He wanted her to feel special.

Dear Angel,

You are my favorite DJ. Your voice is really cute. I hope someday we can meet, but I don't think that will happen. We are too different, so the odds aren't good. Just know when you feel alone or sad that you have a fan.

He didn't sign the letter, and the idea of being cutesy, drawing hearts or stars, made him cringe. He left it open-ended, simply "Love."

Andy copied the address for East Cherokee High onto an envelope. He found it while doing his research online. Then with the envelope hidden under his arm he walked to the convenient store by his home and dropped the letter in a mailbox on the corner. He didn't dare mail it from the house. If his mother came over, which she did nearly every day to write her hate mail, she could find it and ask questions. Her spying was pathological since his father left. After all, his father's affair had started with innocent enough looking letters from a twenty-something grad assistant named Misty Mayberry.

Andy's mother always started with the "Mayberry Letters," when she told the story of her failed first and only marriage. She had experimented with her sob story over years of cocktail parties and card games until she hit upon a structure which was both clear and heartrending. At the end of each retelling she would collapse, chin buried between breasts, and wait for the inevitable open embraces of consolation from her audience. He had seen the show enough to know that she did it for attention, and to hate the fact that unlike him, at one time in her life, she had been in love.

Attraction is a force which draws one body towards another. In physics, force is defined as that which causes one body to accelerate. This acceleration, pulses quickening in ear canals, sweaty palms and dry lips, is a marked sign of attraction we all know. For example, in social dynamics attraction is based largely on propinquity. Propinquity refers to proximity both physically and psychologically. The farther two parties are apart on one or both of those proximities, the less likely they are to attract. Although, anything is possible in this game of chance we call life.

Work at the lottery commission slowed to a halt. For more than a month all the statewide winners had been small-time: twenty dollars here, two hundred dollars there. Small-time winners always cashed their tickets at the gas station or grocery store where they bought them since it made no sense to make a special trip for a pick-three paycheck. This lack of activity left Andy with even more time on his hands than usual. There were details he wanted to attend to which had been pushed away behind theorems that led only to dead ends, and old discoveries long since catalogued and forgotten. At his desk he wrote up an itinerary for his new ventures.

The first new project he had in mind was to formulate a counter argument to Marsha's worldview. He hoped that this would save him the trouble of clearing lottery tickets and newspaper clippings from his desk, and also that it would educate Marsha about the cruel truths of the world. He spent an entire day looking through old news articles online, and printing the most terrible ones out in bold text on bright yellow paper. His research proved that the world was not only random, but malicious.

One article focused on a Florida man who served thirty-five years in federal prison for stealing a television set worth around two hundred dollars at the time he was incarcerated. Another was dedicated to a Michigan teenager who was sentenced to life after being caught with half a joint due to the new "three strikes" law. Each article showed how little sins tied with simple dumb luck and bigotry could destroy a person.

When he had a stack of articles two inches high he clipped them together carefully, and placed them on Marsha's desk for her to read at her leisure.

Andy's second venture began the following Thursday. While his mother let herself in to write a letter of outrage to her congressman about bingo halls, he got down to business in the basement with poster board and silver glitter to make a birthday card for Angel.

On the previous week's show she had mentioned that her birthday was coming up. While she failed to mention the date, he took it as a clue that she wanted some kind of recognition from her audience. A present was out of the question since he feared anything he sent to her would only show how divorced his world was from hers, but he decided a card would do. His mother always liked receiving cards, even from people she couldn't stand, so he guessed Angel wasn't any different.

Angel's card couldn't be store-bought since he always found them to be manufactured and impersonal, so he worked hard on making an original. With the words "Happy Birthday" spelled out in glitter, he stared blankly at the inside flap as her voice came across the airwaves.

"You are listening to East Cherokee High Radio. I'm Angel, a sophomore here at ECH, and I'll be with you all the way up to like the three o'clock hour. Go Tribe!" Splendor. Innocence. The honeyed voice of unrequited love. Andy lost his train of thought and sank into his father's chair, which still smelled like an old man's comb, to listen sincerely.

"I want to thank my biggest fan! Whoever sent me that letter last week was super cool! This song is for you. You rock!" The warm rush of success gushed through his arteries as a band he had never heard of caterwauled into his basement. He hated the music, but the sentiment made him light-headed. The connection was made. Until three o'clock he sat upright with his knees drawn into himself, hoping against hope that she would mention the letter again. She didn't. There was only a laugh, talk about a birthday party, and well wishes for the track team, then silence before the news was read by a junior boy who referred to himself as DJ Al-Mazing.

Andy went back to work on the card. She could be seventeen now he reasoned, almost an adult. Inside the card he printed:

Dear Angel,

Happy Birthday! I think you rock too! Would you like to meet? Give me a clue on the air. Love to meet you.

Love,

A.

He sealed the card up in an envelope decorated with angel stickers, and walked to the mailbox down the street without saying a word to his mother who was stamping fury onto the page with his father's old Companion typewriter.

The law of averages states that eventually everything "evens out." In a lottery eventually someone will win no matter how unlikely the odds simply because of the number of chances taken balanced against the likelihood of any given result. If enough people try to connect with an expected outcome, eventually someone will.

For days Marsha had allowed Andy to work on his projects without interruption. She spoke to him only when necessary. The newspaper articles had ceased to appear in his chair and there were no more lottery tickets taped to the inside of his desk drawers. Their subtle debate over the frequency of implausible success had frozen.

She had also stopped checking up on his progress in regards to charting the locations of winners and amounts received, which was his only true responsibility, so he had stopped filing his reports all together. He never understood the importance of what he did. If the lottery was truly random, he didn't see any reason to keep track of how many tickets were purchased in one area as opposed to another, or why it was vital to log the age, sex, and employment of the claimants. They were empty facts, and he had better things to do with his time. Day after day the figures formed a logjam in his computer, and were left to build without consideration. Angel, on the other hand, was requiring more and more of his time.

She hadn't mentioned his card during her radio show. Andy searched through the recordings he made of every broadcast, but she had given no clue that she had received it or was willing to meet with him. It seemed so disrespectful, and he wanted her to know that. She'd have to explain why she ignored him, she owed him that much, unless something he hadn't factored had gone wrong. Terrible prospects entered his mind.

If she was a cruel girl, a spoiled girl, she could have thrown his card away without a second's thought. She could have shown it to her friends and called him a freak. If it wasn't her fault some teacher could have seen the card, and notified her parents about all the unwanted attention she was getting. They might take her off the air for her own safety, and strand him with only his mother's interruptions for company. Then the most awful thought came; the authorities might be involved. They could skim his DNA from the envelope. They could stake out his home, and ask about all the tapes he'd made. They could interrogate him, and tell his mother about his intentions for girl.

There was nothing left for him to do but wait. He hoped that a sign would come to him down in the basement and ease his nerves. His hard work should be rewarded. He pictured Angel sitting next to him in his car, begging him to understand how important the music of Pontius

Copilot was to her life. He imagined her putting his hand on her leg as they drove away from East Cherokee High toward the endless possibilities ahead.

These ideas sustained him six days a week while other clumsy DJs made their rounds over the airwaves. He made a list of all the things he wanted to ask her when they met. There was so much he could teach her about the universe, and more she could show him about human connections.

It took a few weeks, but Andy lost his job at the lottery commission for gross negligence. His refusal to file his cumulative reports had caused those above him to miss their deadlines. He was given the chance to explain himself, but took the opportunity to rail against the triviality of compiling data for a process that was random. He argued against measuring the demographics of winners since that data could not be used to alter the process itself. His paperwork was a trail of figures that led to nothing. But in the end, arguing for the irrelevance of his job was not the best way to keep it.

Marsha watched him clean out his desk then walked him to the door with an envelope in hand. Andy hoped that it was a severance check, but instead found that it had Marsha's card and lottery tickets for the following week's drawing. He threw it in his car, and drove around the city until sun went down. Then he went home.

At home he found his mother had let herself in again. She sat at the kitchen table and played Bridge with women he did not know. From the door he could hear their debate on the failure rate of modern marriages. She always came to the old house to complain. It held her bitterness.

"Andy come play with us," She said as he walked past them to the stairs. "You never play."

As he made his way up the wooden stairs to his room, he noted that all his mother's friends were divorced. It was the binding tie among them. High-minded men had left them with the corpses of old jackets and filing cabinets. They clung to those things as proof that they had been wronged. At the top of the stairs, he closed the door to his room quietly and lay on his bed to dream about the days to come when his mother's circle of friends would widen even farther. He dreamed of Angel's cue over the air that would bring her to him. They would disappear into the universe, and his mother would be able to have cocktails with new friends who had lost children forever.

The very next Thursday Angel came to him over the airwaves talking in code. "So, I'll be around tomorrow after the three o'clock hour. If anyone wants my autograph or anything, meet me by the soccer field." Andy knew what he had to do.

Scientific brain scans of those in states of deep affection are remarkably similar to those of people with acute mental illness. Love activates the same areas of the mind that are closely linked to biological drives such as drug cravings, thirst, and hunger. Neuroscientists have speculated that this reaction is so akin to the desire for sustenance that without this physiological urge the human race would cease to exist.

Romance for Delinquents

Andy's car idled in the parking lot of East Cherokee High. He had waited since two o'clock, and appreciated that the loss of his job couldn't have come at a better time. He chewed on his shirt sleeve, and thought of all what to say first if he had to say anything at all. Students walked out of the building as time moved on, their eyes on their phones or each other. None of them seemed to be on the verge of adventure. He watched each one with his teeth in his sleeve and salivated.

Around four o'clock the boys' soccer team was running wind sprints out on the field, their faces turning purple as ink blotters. The girls' field hockey team paced back and forth with dangerous clubs in their hands, their skirts lifting and falling while ponytails bobbed. Older men swung weed-eaters along the parking lot as the cars surrounding grew fewer. No bombshell waited with his card in hand. No eager trusting girl scanned the windshields and sidewalks around the school for true romance. There were only athletes and janitors, tired teachers shuffling home and bus drivers back from their runs, everyday people ignorant that change is not only possible, but inevitable. Rules and theories are only context and time.

Sunlight glinted through his windshield and he began to sweat. His face felt as if it was pressed against a light bulb, like he was being interrogated in some bad police show. He was a man sitting alone in a car, waiting for a child to join him in a fairy tale. The heat made him abandon his better judgment.

Inside East Cherokee High, the halls smelled like crepe-paper and French fries. Rumbles came from the band room and the gymnasium, but there was no one in the halls who would notice a man who could have been a substitute teacher walking with paperwork in his hands, and an envelope in his pocket. Hallways led into hallways, a cafeteria at his left, a teachers' lounge to his right. He searched for the studio and marked every exit in case he had to run.

The words "A.V. Room" stood out on a black plaque. The door was unlocked. Inside the switchboard was silent. Headphones hung on hooks next to programming lists that were neatly taped to the wall. He took the envelope marked "For Angel" out from his jacket pocket, and left it in a chair. Then he left the building to drive the secluded side streets past scrap yards and sewage treatment plants toward home.

The following Monday at East Cherokee High the envelope was the topic of discussion. A Latina showed it to all her friends. Some laughed. Other just looked confused. None could guess where it might have come from. Why would anyone leave her an envelope full of lottery tickets?

Angel gave some away to her teachers who thanked her hesitantly. She gave some to her radio advisor, and later at home, divvied up a handful among her uncles and older brothers. The last one she gave to her mother who thanked her as she washed dishes, and watched a telenovela star she was in love with.

The girl knew the lottery tickets were something to be given away. They were no good for her, she was sure of that, because she was only sixteen and too young to win.

There are numerous theories which hope to explain all that exists beyond ourselves, and the vast expanse of time and space. One of the most poetic, I find, is string theory, which proposes that the universe is a constant vibration played in concert with other relative realms of existence. These parallels play in unison like the strings of a violin. Their tremors span the unknown and fill the void as ripples on a pond, or if you like, the breath of mankind as he searches for what he needs most.

The girl's mother switched off the small television set on the counter and stared down at the ticket. On the other side of town, Andy waited in his car in front of a quiet row of newly constructed townhouses. He had been led there by new research, and hoped to better understand the universe at last. There were questions that physics and math couldn't answer.

Dusk fell around him and dimmed the streets. Song birds quietly watched over him from power lines. When he had gathered his notes under his arms, he slowly walked up to a home by the guest parking area and nervously pushed the doorbell. Inside a muffled buzz rang out as he stepped back so that he could be seen through the door. After a few moments, an elderly woman answered.

"Marsha," Andy said quietly, as he stared down at a doormat which featured kittens pawing one another, "I want you to make me happy."

"I don't understand," Marsha said, and for a moment she was considered calling the police.

"I want you to tell me what those articles you left meant," He said as he rolled his father's lecture notes in his hand. "I need to know."

In his perfect sorrow Marsha could find no way to shut him out. The picture of him holding onto the old pile of papers hurt her heart, because she knew he still believed in them. She found herself giving a motherly nod before leading him inside like an orphan.

"Why don't you rest here for a minute. You don't look well."

"I'm not well."

Marsha took his papers and cleared a space for him to sit. She didn't say a word until she made coffee since she prided herself on being a proper host.

"I should leave," he said. "This was a bad idea."

"Then come with me," she replied. Their old debate rekindled an idea inside of her, and she was sure that at last she would win. "It's good to escape from the mind now and then."

"Where do you want to go?"

"Tonight I'm going to teach you about the probability of victory at last," she said. "We'll drive across the river to the gambling boat. I'll teach you to play Poker and Blackjack. This city needs winners. They're all so happy."

Andy lifted himself up to follow her. As she locked the door behind them he quoted an old slogan from the lottery commission. "Somebody has to win."

Little Animals

The cafeteria is quiet. The only exception is a television playing cartoons in the corner, but no one is watching it. Since it is lunchtime, I'm waiting with surgical gloves and a bucket full of detergent for the first patient to vomit. One of them always vomits during meal times. I've worked here long enough to know what to expect. The staff members all believe that they do it on purpose. The directors say they can't help themselves.

I look down the first folding table at the plastic trays— red, blue, yellow, the cheery colors of a Lifesavers roll— and wait for one of the patients to start heaving over their trays. They all eat with plastic spoons that can't be broken. Every day picnic forks aren't allowed since they have points that are sharp and can be broken off. Grocery store picnic knives are banned too. I survey every spoon at the first table and scan down each dirty hand at the second one. They can't take the spoons with them since they can be melted over a heater into a handle with a jagged point. If a patient stuck one of us, which they have in the past, there is no one to complain to. We are the only ones left to deal with them.

I sit down at the second table and hear lips smacking, teeth meeting mush, moans. Outside, past the steel bars, squirrels dart across the lawn. They race up the bird feeder to steal sunflower seeds, then back through the grass and up into the trees chattering things only they can understand. Buses move outside on the street, carrying people back and forth to the city. I smile at the patients next to me but none of them shows any hint of understanding. They never look out the windows.

Behind me a gag turns into a whooping cough then a wave of puke hits the shore of institutional tile below. My eyes close just long enough to forget about blue skies and sunflower seeds before I pull on the gloves and get my bucket. While I start to clean up the mess, Patrick, another care-giver, takes the patient into the shower room to get him cleaned up.

Today it was Billy who threw up his lunch. Tomorrow it will be Davey. The day after that it will be Franky, Timmy, or Suzy. They all have little kid names like that. I wouldn't be able to file a report if the keyboard was missing the Y key. I've started noticing things like that lately.

After I clean up the acrid puddle of half-eaten awful from the floor, I put the bucket back in the kitchen and throw away the gloves. Then I walk down the first table collecting trays. Most of the food here comes in squares. I pick up a red tray with a cube of bile green Jell-O shivering in place. I pick up a blue tray with a meat square on it that looks like Spam, but I know it's not. I pick up yellow trays and green trays until they are all dumped and stacked up for me to clean later.

The patients line up by the kitchen door waiting for dessert. I hand out pudding packs to each one and watch over the line to make sure they sit down with their spoons. Dessert is never solid. When I first started at Evergreen, dessert was a popsicle. That ended after a caregiver named Brenda was stabbed in the face by a Popsicle stick that had been scratched against a brick wall until it came to a point. Now they get pudding packs and soft serve ice cream.

After I hand out the last dessert, I lock the kitchen behind me and wait for Patrick to come back so I can take Jimmy his lunch. Jimmy can't eat with the others since he is in permanent isolation.

Patrick comes back from the shower room with Billy and we give him a pudding pack. Then I go back to the kitchen and lock the door behind me out of habit. The kitchen is one of the few places at Evergreen we truly control. Patients aren't allowed in it since there are too many nasty things to work with. There are sharp butcher knives on chains that hang from the counter. There is bug spray, carving forks, and an industrial can opener. There are gas burners that could be turned on unlit. The kitchen is our safe room.

I pull Jimmy's boxed lunch out of the refrigerator and open the door that goes back into the main dining room. Patrick is standing with his shoulders hunched up, his finger pointing out towards the back of the room.

"Kenny's about to go," he says under his breath. His other hand reaches down to his hip out of habit, but there's not a gun there anymore. He hasn't been a cop since he killed a kid. At least that's what he says. Here we aren't allowed as much as a stun gun.

"Wait for it," I say. I sit the box lunch down by the kitchen door and we both start moving slowly towards the back of the dining hall.

Kenny is a huge mangle of muscle and fear. He could be forty, or sixty, or twenty-five. It's impossible to tell how old most of them are. Their bodies run on different clocks. We are a good ten feet away when it happens. He starts making a sound like "CH! CH! CH!" and then starts to bawl and howl while swinging his arms around like bicycle chains directed at what he sees that isn't there.

When he jumps we jump.

Patrick grabs one arm and I grab the other, then we let our feet leave the floor so that we're dead weight on either side. Kenny howls even more and stomps his feet against the floor. I get my footing and pull hard to one side. Patrick feels the shift and follows up with a push on his side. We've done this a hundred times. We all hit the floor hard.

Kenny starts to cry and shudder. We sit behind him and wait

for it to end. We aren't allowed to use the plastic handcuffs that look like garbage ties anymore because they leave marks on a struggling patient. We have to just sit with him until he calms down and we can move him back to his room. I look up at the clock and feel my arms start to cramp. Inside my mouth there is a sore that's been growing for two weeks.

An hour passes, and Kenny is back in his room. I leave Patrick to change Kenny's diaper and take him to the shower room to clean up. I'm sure that I'm losing my hair. Every time I cough it's cancer. I can't sleep anymore. My nose has been bleeding for no reason. The general practitioner that comes by here said it's all in my head. He says that I just need to relax and take some time off, maybe just go upstate for a while, but I don't think that will help.

I put hydrogen peroxide on my arm where Kenny's nails dug in and go back to get Jimmy's lunch. I hate feeding him off-schedule. It makes him worse.

Jimmy's room is on the fourth floor next to storage rooms for toilet paper rolls and bed sheets. When he first came here he was put in general population, but that didn't work out. He was too violent and they could never get his medication right. Eventually they just put him up at the top where he couldn't bite off fingers and claw anyone's eyes out. He sits up there day after day waiting for me.

I count each step as I make my way up the stairs with his lunch. I have an apple in my pocket as a peace offering. He loves apples. It's one of the few words he can say. Most of his speech comes out in growls and hisses. I was told once that his mother was a speed freak who got knocked up by some psycho. We have a lot of patients who were born scrambled eggs thanks to crackhead mothers. We have even more that were pimped out as kids, kicked around like soda cans. But I never read the patient's files. I only hear rumors. I don't try to explain Jimmy.

When I get to the fourth floor I stop to catch my breath. I want to set myself for feeding time. If I'm holding anything under the surface, he'll know. I want to open the door smiling. He can feel whatever crawls around inside you. He knows nothing else but that. You have to be there for him or he goes off. You have to watch him eat until he's finished. If you don't give yourself fully you're a target. It's a small thing to ask— consideration.

Jimmy likes me. I'm the only one who can get near him except for the psychiatrist, Doctor Pacific. I feed him after the doctor medicates him. We each make our way up the stairs three times a day. Our lives are wearing down to this. I put a fake smile on my face like a stewardess and unlock the door.

When I walk in, he's in the shadows under the window. It's his favorite spot, his back to the outside world that passes him by. For a second I stand still so he can size me up. His smashed mind takes time to put the pieces together, so three times a day I wait like this. After a minute he starts.

"Abbbul, Appbuhhl." He walks over to me wide-eyed, taking his time. He needs a shave. He creeps towards me with his hands out.

He wears a big fake smile too.

The box is on the floor at his feet. He sits on his mattress and pokes his finger into one square thing or another. Jell-O splatters onto his scraggly beard. He eats the squares in fistfuls without looking up at me. He knows he doesn't get the apple until all the food is gone. That can take almost an hour depending on his mood.

So he sits and digs his fingers into the box lunch and I spin a quarter on its end from where I sit on the other side of the room. The sun is bright and I think about stream-fed lakes and mountains, warm places I've never been. I think about walking away from the walled-in planet. But I can hear him slurping and gnashing in the corner. If I wasn't here, who would take care of him?

"You need a shave Jimmy." The hair on his face grows funny. It pops up in patches and is real thin so he looks like a middle-school kid trying to flaunt puberty. He must be thirty. Or he could be seventeen.

"They say it took six cops to bring you in the last time Jimmy. They say you killed a bunch of stray cats." He stabs his fingernail into a gray square that comes in a box marked "pre-portioned gravy." "The Doctor says he can't pump enough juice into you to get you back to a real hospital." Jimmy pushes his tray to the side with his foot and slides on his knees to where I sit.

"Aahhhppul. Appprrllhh." His eyes are blown wide and black with anticipation. I toss the apple to him and he moves back to the mattress where he can tear into it in peace. It's always this way. He's on his side. I'm on mine. No one gets hurt.

The fruit's skin is torn away with a hundred little fingernail flips.

I look at the way he uses his nails on the apple and worry about the next time I'll have to cut them. Jimmy tore a caregiver's earlobe off before I came here. I've heard he's done worse. When it comes time to groom him again I'll have to do the clipping.

Jimmy wouldn't be here if he was a patient that the state of New Jersey deemed manageable. All the patients at Evergreen are here because they are too violent to be housed in any state-run mental hospital. When the state can't handle a person, they turn them over to our company. It keeps them from worrying about liability lawsuits I guess. They give us the biters, fighters, breakers, rapists, and we store them away.

I start spinning the quarter again and watch Jimmy finish off his apple ritual. When he's chewed his way down to the core he starts picking out the little black seeds one by one and puts them under his pillow. He wants this to be a secret since he only does it when he thinks I'm not watching. When all the seeds are taken out he slides back over to me and hands me the core. He smiles and I smile. That's the dance.

The door locks as I leave. I have ten more hours before I can go home. I forget what day it is anymore. I work in a submarine. Every day is this day.

By the afternoon, I'm in the office next to the dining room entering incident reports into the computer. One reads, "Patient Alvarez threw feces onto caregiver Joyce and began to seizure." Another one reads, "Patient Harris was found bleeding from the anus in the third floor hallway and taken to infirmary." I enter the times and dates, names of staff members and attendants.

I've been adding editorials to the reports. I write that patient Schneider is one mean motherfucker. I haven't held back any details. If a patient calls a caregiver a "cocksucker" that's what I write instead of "an obscenity." No one reads these reports anyway.

When the reports are finished I start writing letters to the patients' families, if they have any. I have to write polite letters about how well their son or daughter is doing, and go on about their art projects or friends here. Then I put down what each patient needs. Kenny needs four triple-X large sweatshirts and some new sweatpants. Jamey needs a new bra since her old one is too tight. I sign each letter with a different name. I doubt any of the letters will be answered.

The families of the people here only come around on Christmas, if they come around at all. Some of the parents are in prison, some are dead. Most don't care what happens to their kid one way or the other. I write "Jimmy needs new shoes" on the last letter and sign it illegibly. It's going somewhere on the Lower East Side to a woman named Dotty. It will probably end up at a dead letter office or in a recycling bin. I've never gotten a response. These letters make me glad I grew up in an orphanage instead of being shipped around like the foster kids are. At least in an orphanage you stop believing you'll get picked out by the time you know there's no Santa Claus.

Patrick only comes around once the office work is done. He leaves the typing to me and I leave the wrestling to him when I can. He's stronger than I am, and I think he likes it anyway.

"What do you think he is?" Patrick asks pointing to the letter addressed to Dotty, Jimmy's mother.

"What do you mean?" I ask.

"You think he's Puerto Rican, Cambodian, Italian?"

"I don't know," I say. "I never thought of him being anything."

"He's probably a mongrel," Patrick says, pointing at the address. "They're all mongrels down there."

"What's that supposed to mean?" I ask.

"Nothing," Patrick says.

Three purple dents stand out on Patrick's elbow when he rolls up his sleeve. He says if he hadn't had help, Jimmy's teeth would have made it all the way to the bone and left him a cripple. He tells me I don't know what he is capable of since I've only heard the stories. Jimmy has taken off ears, blinded nurses, but I only get to see him after the drugs hit him.

Patrick has another mark on his arm, a tattoo that's spreading out under his skin real bad to the point that I can hardly tell what it says. I can make out the blurry pin-up girl above the writing on it, but the words all smear together until I can only read "And Run." I don't trust him.

The volume on the television goes up real high all at once, and Patrick spins around towards a huddle of four patients shoving each other in front of the set. He sprints like a German Shepherd and grabs the first one he sees by the shoulder, jerking him back and moving on to the next. I don't think he was ever a cop. I think he was a security guard. I don't think anyone would have ever given him a gun.

The volume on the television set goes back down and Patrick

puts each of the patients in separate corners to cool down.

Doctor Pacific comes in and gets the letters to send out with the rest of the mail. He looks young, he could be my age, and I wonder why he works here.

"I don't know why you bother sending those," I offer with my feet up on the desk like I'm real important.

"Company policy," the Doctor says. "There's always hope someone cares more about their child than their check."

"The families get a check?" I always assumed the state got the money for the patients and then sent it to our company. I forget about families.

"They get a nice check," he says. "If your DNA is garbled enough and you can keep making flawed little babies, you could have a check big enough to retire in Tahiti." He says this straight-faced. Everything he says is that way, to the point and a little depressing.

"How come they never visit then?" I ask, already knowing why.

"Because they don't care. If anyone did, I'd send their child home with them rules or no rules. Care is something every patient needs, but few find in an institution. I can't imagine leaving one of my children like this. We all need love, especially the broken." He looks at the patients in the corners of the room then out the window. I just nod.

"Filed away," I say. "No mamas here."

"Well," the Doctor says, "it's almost time to give Jimmy his medicine." I'm the only one he mentions Jimmy to. I'm sure of that most of the other caregivers don't even know he exists. At this point he's mostly paperwork anyway.

"What's he up to on his meds?" I ask. I don't know what's a little or a lot, but it's good to have someone on the inside to talk to.

"More than I should give him, but less than he needs. He gets more tolerant every week." Doctor Pacific sets the letters down again. The thought of going up there is on his face.

"Is what they say true? Did it really take six cops to drag him in the last time?"

"No. Seven or eight. I forget. When he's unmedicated he's a time bomb. He'd kill anything in sight. But it's not his fault." Doctor Pacific pulls up a plastic office chair beside me. I look at Patrick playing big man by the television. That's all he can control. Little things.

Doctor Pacific gets real serious and says, "Do you remember your dreams?"

I shake my head.

"Never?" he asks.

I nod yes. I don't remember anything when I'm not here.

"Well you see the thing about dreams is there is no logic to them. Everything is completely valid without context or reason. Nothing ties into anything else. Every event mutates into another world or time without logic. That's what Jimmy's mind is like with everything except for us. He's found a way to tie us down inside."

I don't say anything. I feel a frozen eight-ball rolling inside my head from missing too much sleep and eating pre-portioned squares. The practitioner said that my body is trying to tell me something; that I should listen to it and take some time off.

"If he connected one other thing from the world outside himself, I'd set him free today." Doctor Pacific crossed his legs and moved the files around with two fingers. "It would be amazing, an improvement like that, but you know in real life people don't spring up from decades-long comas, and individuals like Jimmy don't get better. Especially without the real care of a family."

"So you think if he had any real parents it would make any difference?" Never having had parents made it easy to imagine that they had super powers. When I was in the orphanage I almost died from the pneumonia. After I got better one of the church ladies who volunteered took credit for my recovery since she'd held my hand all night, said that all I needed all along was a real mother's touch. I spent years wondering if I almost died, not because of the flu, but because I didn't have a mother."

"I have to give him his meds." Doctor Pacific straightens his back and heads towards the door.

Patrick is tired of playing crossing guard to a parking lot so he lets the patients start milling around again. I see him smile a big dumb gorilla smile to himself as he makes his way back to the office. Caregivers like him always stay the longest.

"Hey Doc," he yells. "How come you ended up here anyway?"

Doctor Pacific feels the same way about Patrick that I do. He picks up the letters and makes his way towards the door.

"I'm a psychiatrist," he says seriously. "Patients in private practice lie to you. They make up things so they don't sound so bad at the end of the day. Here some can't talk at all, and it's for the better."

He makes his way through the doors to give Jimmy his medicine. I spend the next two hours looking out the window at the bus route and the sun dying against New York City.

Five o'clock I get Jimmy's dinner out of the refrigerator and leave Patrick to deal with the rest of them. In one pocket I have an apple and in the other I have a little pink razor. It's the kind where the blade isn't so sharp. It's made for women to use on their legs. I brought a hand mirror, but no nail clippers. One thing at a time.

At the top of the stairs my belly is full of battery acid. I don't care what my last check-up said. I'm sure I have an ulcer. It's not that I don't want to see all those trees and lakes they keep suggesting. It's just that there's no way to get to them now.

I unlock Jimmy's door and stand there waiting for him to notice me. He's not waiting for me in his spot. He's on his knees by the window. There's something gray and brown on the other side of the bars. He moves one hand under his pillow then back to the window, mumbling gleefully to himself. I see a tail, then two black eyes. Little claws from the outside world waiting for apple seeds. Then the squirrel is gone.

The whole time Jimmy eats his dinner I look out the window. I wonder if I left it open or if the doctor did. I watch him eat and try to picture what food looks like in his world. What made apple seeds and squirrels come together in a way that added up in his mind?

After he finishes his dinner, I move over slow and show him the razor and the mirror. His eyes glass over and he starts to hiss. I check his hands but they're not curling up yet. They hang over his knees and I get the impression he's waiting for me to bargain. I show Jimmy the apple.

He takes it and slides back on the mattress. As finger-flips of apple peel fly away I start to shave the sides of his face. He doesn't fight. I get as much as I can before he moves from fingers to teeth.

The squirrel understands Jimmy. Jimmy understands the squirrel. I think about how long it must have taken him to train it, about how he was being kind and nurturing to something so small and easy to break. Maybe the doctor was wrong. Maybe comas can end. I wonder what I should do next.

When he hands me the core, I put it with the empty dinner box and show him the mirror. He has no idea what he's looking at. He hasn't tied himself down.

It had been five weeks since my last day off, so Evergreen made me take one whether I wanted to or not. But I'm no good outside anymore. I go to movies and wander around supermarkets. I catch the bus at the stop out front of the institution and ride around the city until I can come back inside. It's hard to talk to people on the outside. All my stories are about rape and diapers, someone getting their nose bitten off. Things no one wants to know.

When I come back to Evergreen it's late in the evening. I'm not due until midnight but I've got nowhere else to go. Patrick is smiling and shows me a shoebox.

"You missed it," he says. "Dotty came."

"Who's Dotty?" I ask. He's laughing. I hate the way he laughs.

"Jimmy's mom or something," he says and he shows me the form she signed to check in. "I don't think she's going to live long."

"What are you talking about?" This only happened because I left and Patrick was here. Things fall apart without me. What did he say to her?

"Junky shakes. Believe me I've seen them. Her skin was poked through with purple sores, starting to turn green already. Real mess. Made me glad she didn't see him." He walks to the kitchen. There are no patients in the dining hall. I know he's left them locked in their rooms all day.

"She didn't even see him?" I ask.

"I mean she wanted to. Said she'd come to take him home. Walk him back in new shoes or something. She was talking fast and I wasn't listening anyway."

"Why didn't you let her see her son?"

"I'm not going up there," Patrick said, "and I don't have time for some meth head and psychopath reunion."

"You should have let him go with her."

"You're right. It would have saved us the trouble of dealing with that little animal. Maybe next time I will. But anyway that's not the best part. The shoes she brought weren't even the right size. One was a ten and the other was eleven. It's like she didn't even try. You wrote nine down didn't you?"

"Yeah," I say. "But it doesn't make a difference." I take the box from Patrick and sit it by the trash on my way to the kitchen. He leaves for the night and I wonder if Jimmy noticed that the shoes didn't fit. I wonder if they fed him while I was gone.

I walk up the stairs. The smoke detectors chirp like starlings every sixty seconds, just one note, then quiet. I make my way to the fourth floor and unlock Jimmy's door. He's awake and waiting by the window with his seeds. I look at his shoes. They're knock-off running shoes without the laces. He can't run in a place like this.

His hands move slowly over the food I brought him. In the moonlight I can see the doctor must have tried to cut his nails. He should have known to leave it to me. His fingers are a bloody mess. He fights when he doesn't have time to put things together, when things get new.

"This happens when I'm away," I say as he plods his tender fingers over the food. "This happens when he's here."

After a long time he finishes eating and puts his grimy hands up for an apple, but I don't have one. I was thinking about the shoes and forgot about the squirrels. I walk him through the door and towards the stairs. No one else is on. I want to feed the squirrels too.

At the bottom of the stairs I lead him through the hallways towards the dining room. Then I unlock the kitchen door and lead him inside.

"Apppullb," he coughs and blurts. I sit down with an apple and a knife. Without his fingernails I have to peel it for him. He watches the skin fall away from the fruit and his teeth start to chatter.

He palms the bare apple to his teeth and tears into it. I don't watch him. I don't like to. I look at his feet and think that Patrick should have said something about the shoes. He should have led Dotty up the stairs, and given her back her son. I get the shoebox to check for clues.

The shoebox has a label on it with the same address I send the letters to. It has our address too. I wonder why Dotty didn't mail it. Maybe she thought coming here was her last chance. She wanted to see her son. He has a mother out there and she wanted to see her son. She cared.

I give Jimmy a plastic spoon and teach him to pick apple seeds out with it. Then I take him upstairs to get dressed.

Outside the night is cold and quiet. It's the kind of night that makes you feel that you don't deserve to be so alone. I look at the city waiting out in the distance all lit up and ugly, and think of Dotty. I think of all the happy people who never have to know what I know, about the buses that take them home to mothers who love them.

We're waiting outside the gate. I'm holding Jimmy's hand. I know this is the right bus line. Jimmy needs his mother. He has to have the chance. He looks tired. He is off schedule and the medicine is wearing down. I pull his collar up and straighten his hair.

When the bus comes I move him through the door carefully, holding him by the shoulders. We take baby steps toward the back of the bus. Jimmy mutters to himself, shivers under his shirt, but no one on the bus lifts their heads to notice us. They are alone and reverent to that fact. We are alone too.

Dotty will teach him all the things I never got the chance to know.

We sit down in the very last seat. Jimmy slides his hand to the emergency door, but I gently move his arms into his lap as the bus' air breaks release and we pull away from the gates of Evergreen. He's not fighting me yet, only looking out the window at places he's never seen.

The world in his mind must be moving now. The chemicals disintegrating in his bloodstream are losing their hold. I know that soon he will have to make a choice about how he feels about all this motion. I pull him close to me and watch the city lights grow brighter. My arm cradles his shoulder as his shakes grow worse, as his hands ball into fists. My other hand trails out the window, dropping apple seeds onto the concrete beneath us.

There are trees in Central Park and a lake too. By morning I'll sit under their branches and watch toy boats float across the water. By then Jimmy will be in his mother's arms.

Boys and Girls in Motels

The Cozy Motel, Kentucky

The only place to stay in town was a sagging platform of concrete and plaster which flattened out the top of an auto parts store. It was a business passed down in the family, changing hands like a grandfather clock or a box of photographs from one member to another. Out-of-towners who stayed there found ironed sheets, clean towels, and Bibles left by Gideons and worn by those in need. It was an honest place.

In the car the boy sat next to his first girlfriend while his uncle drove them to the wrestling show. They hurried to see heroes from parts unknown beat evil clowns and convicts senseless under the thunder of hard rock. In the backseat the girl painted the boy's face like his hero with mustard and a napkin while she hummed along to the radio.

"The Macho Killer is going to be there tonight," the boy said as he fished a fry from his Happy Meal bag. "He hates King Leonard because they used to be friends."

"He ain't no Macho Killer," the boy's uncle said. "He used to stay at The Cozy when him and his brother Lonnie wrestled Smokey Mountain. I threw them out for stealing towels."

The girl wiped her nose and admired her work. "What about his girlfriend?"

"Miss Divine?" The boy's uncle asked as he changed lanes. "She was a real beauty that one. Classy."

"You met Miss Divine?" The two yelped together as their young hearts lifted at the thought of a beauty queen sleeping in one of the rooms where they played murder.

"I sure did," he began again. "They say she was a dancer. You can tell by a woman's feet. Dancers have ugly feet."

"You saw her feet?" The boy asked, winding a foam championship belt around his waist.

"No," he said, "but she moved like a dancer. The other two stayed passed out drunk."

That night the children screamed louder than they had ever before in their lives. They had a first-hand account that the heel Macho Killer was a real villain—a towel thief.

The Resting Pine, Arizona

When they left California the girl took her pants off in the car. There was no air-conditioner, and the heat struck her in waves as they passed through the mountains.

The boy had never driven a stick-shift before so they had to depend on long runs. If he hit a stoplight they were lost. Roadside flea-markets bled into fruit stands near Barstow, and afterwards they vanished into the Mojave at seventy miles an hour.

In the car they had a change of clothes, sodas, and an ounce of sticky weed to make the drive a daydream. The girl had spent months stealing matchbooks from diners for the drive. In her opinion matchbooks were like socks; a person could never have too many.

By the end of the day the desert had disappeared. The car came to a stop in Flagstaff, a city surrounded by timberland seven-thousand feet above sea level. He promised to find her a hot shower and something vegetarian to eat.

They had made it through the first day, and already the boy saw her in a different light. She was softer than he remembered, innocent. It seemed to him the more a person loves somebody the more they change them.

The lobby of the motel was decorated with statuettes of Hindu deities. Above the front desk curling blue arms spread out like a crab behind black-bodied goddesses heavy with jewels. They signed in under fake names and paid in cash.

In the evening the boy sat on the floor in his underwear and watched her sleep while the television played a documentary about the Mississippi River. Hernando Desoto first laid eyes on it in 1541, when he was forty-four years old. Days later they would jet across it. They were young. They were explorers too.

Cherry Blossom Motel, Georgia

The manager led the boy to a room on the second floor by the vending machine, but left before he knocked. He had his own problems to deal with.

In a moment a pregnant girl pushed open the flaked green door just enough to see who could be knocking. She took care to only crack it open only so far since they were alone, and she didn't want to disturb her grandmother on the bed. In the distance an ambulance whined down the street for the third time that morning.

"Do you own a blue Ford?" The boy asked with his hands at his sides, but was answered with silence. "The manager said it was yours."

In the room the girl's grandmother flipped through the pages of a family album until they turned blank then started again.

"I hit your car in the parking lot," the boy said. "It's not bad, but you should come and see." Staring down at the hump hanging low from the girl's midsection made him feel worse.

"It's not my car," the girl answered patiently. "It's my grandmother's. Is it bad?"

"No, it's a dent. Not even. You should see." He stepped back from the door.

"Then you should go. It will be fine." Her fingers curled away from the door as it moved to cover her face.

"No. I have insurance. I hit it."

"Go home," the girl pleaded under her breath. "She won't understand anyway."

Inside the girl walked back to the bed, and slowly eased herself down next to her grandmother. She put the album on her lap, and started over again from page one while her grandmother concentrated. "This is Sharon," the girl said as she put her finger on the first picture. "She is my mother, your oldest girl. She is the one waiting for you."

Stay Inn, Utah

The Mormon College had rules for young souls. It had always been that way. There were rules against holding hands or kissing in public. There were rules against wearing beer company shirts, pierced noses, and blue hair. There were rules to keep the students in place.

Each student had two overnight passes a semester which had

to be signed by their parents. If a student left without an overnight pass they were expelled. The college had learned long ago that it was easier to cast off troublemakers than to try and reform them. A dozen went home each semester, and the sight of angry parents packing cars with cardboard boxes sent the right message.

The night before finals the boy in the Jack Daniel's shirt sat in a Denny's with a girl he had known for a week. He had met her in art class where she only painted dead trees encircled by nursery rhymes written backwards. Together they smoked cigarettes and drank coffee. Without their passes they sank down into their vinyl seats each time the door opened.

"I've got this song I've been working on," the boy said. "When I get a guitar I'll play it for you."

"Do you know how to play?" The girl asked as she unscrewed the cap from the salt shaker.

"I can learn," the boy said. "God knows I have the time here."

They spent the night together in a motel set for demolition across from the restaurant. The television set was broken. The polyester comforter was stained with motor oil. At the window the boy watched bulldozers pull down the mountain across from them in the dark while ladybugs explored the gaps in the blinds. Together they made love as if there was no hope left for them tomorrow.

***

Romance for Delinquents

Golden Motor Court, Oregon

Sitting at a card table the soldier talked about the last car he owned. There was no right way to start. The girl scratched underneath her wig and watched raindrops ink down the window. Outside the weather was taking a turn for the worse. She had nowhere else to be until it cleared, and in the end it was his money anyway.

"They were debriefing all of us on Guam, but there was nothing to tell them that they didn't already know. I had this car waiting for me on the island the whole time I was over there. I used to dream about it when it was too hot to sleep. It was a Vette. God knows who got it on the island in the first place." With his good hand he took a drink of bourbon from the bottle in front of him, and a look cast across his face as he was suddenly grasped by a powerful idea, one which had to be considered as it was sure to evaporate with his next breath.

She hated the soldiers when they came back. Their kind of empty was different from hers, but she thought they should have been able to meet on common ground since they had both seen the world as it is. In the end they all made her feel like a poor stand-in for lost loves. When they reached for her tremors moved down their arms as if she had a mind full of bullets for them.

She stood as he talked about brown tree snakes choking the engines of transport planes, and began to undress in the corner. The light switched off behind her, and filled the room with blocks of red and gray.

"When I came back to the island it was a wreck. The salt water in the air had rusted the fenders off of it. It was the only thing I missed, and when I came back it was full of holes."

In the dark she struggled to find her bearings before she reached his lips. "Don't you want to play?" she asked as her hands caressed the divots and burn marks that covered his cheek.

"I want you to know," the boy said as he moved her hand to his chest, "I'm a real good man when I'm home."

The Steer Inn, Texas

The little girl sat on the toilet in the bathroom and watched her mother rub petroleum jelly across her teeth until they shined like piano keys. Next to her on the sink sat a roll of duct tape and a bottle of vegetable oil. By the door a plastic tackle box was filled with lipstick, eye liner, blush, foundation, and curlers. Her mother called it her "beauty box."

"Now watch Mama," her mother said as she wrapped duct tape around her midsection and underneath her breasts. "See how they pop up now?"

The little girl nodded and handed her the vegetable oil.

"You have to shine princess," she said as she greased up her bare legs. "The judges want to see you sparkle."

"You look like a princess Mama," the little girl said as she strained to make her feet touch a crack in the tile floor, and wished that she had cowboy boots.

"No honey, you're the princess," she corrected as her daughter turned to tug at the wallpaper where it sagged free above her. "Now go wait outside with your brother." Alone she swallowed diet pills and took an enema before finishing her make-up. Then she pulled a garment bag off the shower rod and held her gown in front of her. "A queen."

When she had blossomed she walked out of the bathroom in her sparkling dress and waited for applause. The little girl sprang from the bed with her hands slapping together, then stood next to her mother in a Junior Miss pose.

Under the sheets the boy with the dirty face played his video game and ignored them both.

"Honey," the mother called. "Tell us we're beautiful."

"I've almost got him beat," he said.

"Say it!" The little girl yelled as she pulled the sheets off, and swiped his game to the floor.

The boy ran his fingers through his uncombed hair and looked up at the meanest smiles in the world. "You're beautiful."

The Home For Wayward Celebrities

    To the weekend pilots above, Tiff's broken down hatchback must have looked like a giant beetle; one that had been attacked by bumper stickers before being turned belly-up in the sun. On the other hand, since their single engine planes were low enough in the sky to bring the cliff into view, they might have been reminded of *The Wizard of Oz* since at that moment Tiff's legs stuck out from underneath the jacked-up wreck as if some cruel tornado had dropped it on her from altitude. While the engines of their Cessnas sang like hummingbirds above a sea spotted with sailboats carrying adventurers to Santa Barbara or Catalina, Gabriel could only watch them pass by and regret the fact that they were too high above him to be bothered with his questions.

Standing on the edge of the scenic overlook he wanted desperately to ask the pilots how he looked on the rocks below them, and secretly hoped that they would see his standing on the edge of the cliff next to a broken down Mazda as a metaphor. He wanted to ask them where exactly he was at this place in time, believing that they would have the answers since it always seemed as if solutions came from those above him. But half a mile below there was no hope. Only the seals that sunned themselves on the rocks beneath the cliff gave any notice to his existence. He was stranded. There was nothing for him to do but to try and piece together what had happened to him during the last twenty-four hours.

Walking back toward the car, he noticed that Stella still sat in the passenger seat as rigid as she had been before when they were all on the road. It was a hundred degrees inside the car, but she would not break her pose if only to roll down the window or wipe the sweat from her brow. Her composure only added to his discomfort. Underneath the car, Tiff's legs jerked and bowed as she swore. He had known both women for exactly twelve hours.

To come to terms with his place in time, Gabriel closed his eyes and tried to recall the last thing he did before walking to the edge of the scenic overlook. Each moment of his life was a link in a chain, one bead on a string of pearls, a drop of rain filling the well of his life. He began to work backwards through each one so that he could find his way into the present. This was a technique he had learned in therapy when at eleven years old he had run away from home for the first time. He had been told by professionals that each day in his life was a photograph, a subconscious entry left unexamined, and that the only way to understand his choices was to pull memories out one by one and study their value. Behind him, Tiff swore at a seagull that had come to check in on her progress.

Walking backwards through time in the breeze, Gabriel saw himself exiting the car after it had skated off the Pacific Coast Highway an hour south of Ventura before resting on the side of the road. The moment before the breakdown, Tiff's Mazda's engine sounded the way a dryer would sound if someone threw a handful of nickels in with their wash. Moving to the time before that, he saw the sun rising over scrub-brush spotted mountain tops. The hours that filled the night before the sunrise were a line of headlights. In the car the two women did not bother to make conversation with one another. They rode along in their roles. Stella, the silent sage of an era which had long since disappeared, looking ever forward through her glasses, and Tiff lighting cigarette after cigarette as she pushed the Mazda's accelerator to the floor and hoped for the best. Gabriel could only remember scraps from the rest of their drive: oil rigs blinking offshore like sinking castles, a bonfire burning to cinders in the sand, and two women walking up to him on the beach. Rooted in the now, Gabriel begins again.

"How does it look?" The feet below him twisted half moons into the gravel.

"Bad," Tiff replied. "I don't know what I was hoping for." In the backseat Stella fiddled with her pocketbook and adjusted her legs quietly on the seat.

"We should let her out," Gabriel said as he pressed his hand against the window. Although it was still early in the day the glass felt like an oven door.

"She'll be fine," Tiff said. "If she gets out without another driver she'll only be confused." With that Tiff drug herself out from underneath the car and dusted off her legs before slowly lowering the jack to let the hatchback level out again. "I have to call someone."

Gabriel opened the door and sat in the backseat with Stella. He watched Tiff pace nervously around the front of the car before settling on the hood with a cell phone pressed to her ear.

Sweat misted underneath the crown of gray curls which hung loose where they had worked free from Stella's ponytail. Gabriel smiled in her direction and tried again to paste her in the landscape of television myths. She was a star, if a dim and dying light, but he had no way to find her place in the cosmos this early in the morning. He gathered that she had no map for herself either by the way her hands remained folded patiently on her purse.

"I have a driver." That was all Tiff would share. Her plans were her own and Gabriel was only there to assist. When the money came he could leave this day behind, and never worry about the ramifications of his action ricocheting through space. He believed that if he stayed in motion long enough Karma, or whatever sense of hapless justice one ascribed to, would never be able to find him. Since he was a child he had been running. The ties that bound everyday people, the invisible cords of family and place, had been worn threadbare by his drifting.

A day ago he had been dropped off by a trucker who spoke broken English. The man had picked him up on the side of the highway and driven him south before the time came to turn his tanker inland toward the miles of irrigated alfalfa and strawberry fields that spread out toward the mountains. Gabriel had spent the drive memorizing lines from *Sunset Boulevard* from a bent paperback he had purchased days earlier in San Francisco for a dollar. When he arrived in Los Angeles he wanted to be prepared. He imagined that to be an actor was to be full of dialogue and devoid of expectations. When he exited the truck he gave the driver a "thumbs up" which made him feel like a silly figure out of a road movie: dumb, young, and uniquely American.

The day before in Monterey the sun had been high in the sky. No rain had fallen in over a month and the lawns surrounding him had dried to the color of khaki slacks. Now in the car, sipping ice water from a thermos Tiff had taken out from underneath the driver seat, he pulled the memories of the day before out to appreciate them.

The first image was of a young mother who sat next to her friend on a bench outside a Ralph's Supermarket and mentioned that it was only a matter of time until the whole state caught fire again. The dried scrub brush surrounding the highways would snag a flicker from a cigarette thrown from a passing car and the hills would become an inferno. She kept her eyes on the horizon waiting for the first trails of smoke to appear.

Her friend argued that wasn't necessarily the case. She thought that the rains would come soon and that the highways were doomed to be buried by mudslides. She imagined the National Guard digging out SUVs and tour buses for weeks while news anchors reported on their efforts. The women shared an ice cream cone as they nudged a stroller with their feet and debated which disaster would doom them first. Together they seemed to regret the fact that on that lazy afternoon they had nothing to fear.

Stella began to sing a song to herself from the backseat. Tiff took the thermos from Gabriel and drank the last of the water before reassuring him that the new driver was on his way. "You'll like him," she said. "He's a real cowboy."

"What is she singing?" Gabriel asked.

"I'm not sure," Tiff answered as she opened her door so that the breeze could cool them off. "Probably something from *The King and I*."

Gabriel closed his eyes and concentrated on the song that brushed against his ears, its soft tones lulling him back to the night before on the beach.

When he first saw the flames rising up from the sands he thought that the mother's premonition had come true. Past the thin gray blades of sea grass and over the tortoise-shell stones he could see smoke rising into the night while black figures danced around in the glow. Stumbling over the rocky shore that buffered the sea from civilization he walked toward the tide.

It was a celebration in the darkness. Boys in college T-shirts and Hawaiian shorts danced in crooked steps while music played from a stereo out of sight. Girls huddled together with their backs to the wind and pushed their toes into the wet sand as they watched the boys gyrate. In the center of the group a bonfire kicked sparks into the sky sending embers across the universe. Gabriel sat on his backpack and watched the scene play out, happy to have stumbled onto a private frenzy. That was when he met the two who would take him south.

Gabriel ran away from home for the second time when he was thirteen, and made it as far as Memphis. When he ran out of money and options he called his parents. They arrived before the morning came and found him lying on the sidewalk in front of a Greyhound bus station asleep. His mother would tell him years later how peaceful he looked, and how she mourned the fact that they couldn't just leave him there. "You were humming in your sleep," she had told him. "You just looked serene. I wanted to take you to Graceland." He spent the following three months in a group home for troubled boys where in day-long therapy sessions he sat in a circle of folding chairs and was begged to answer the question, "Why?"

Stella hadn't spoken, but she hardly needed to. Tiff offered opinions and explanations for her as if she was speaking for a deaf baby sister. It was clear that Stella was in trouble, or would be if she didn't get home, and it was in her silent distress that Tiff had found opportunity.

Gabriel had taken the women for ghosts when he first saw them moving from the shadows of the beach toward him. Tiff's stout body moved with caution over the seawall. Stella followed behind her, her head covered with a shawl. Hand in hand they made their way to him without recognition, and at such a late hour it was easy to believe that they would spirit him away. They did.

Tiff spoke first that night. "Are you alone?" she asked. "Do you need money?"

"I'm watching the fire," Gabriel answered.

"Would you like to make some money though?" Tiff asked again. Her arms cradled Stella.

"What do you want?"

"I need a goat," Tiff replied with a wink. Ten minutes later they were on their way. Inside the car Stella lifted the shawl from her head and let her gaze settle onto her guest. "Stella, this is your grandson," Tiff said. "He is here to help you." Stella blew a kiss to him, and they sped away.

The sun climbed high above the broken down Mazda, and inside the three grew anxious. Stella had long since finished singing the songs she could recall. She sat blank-faced while her thin body sank into the vinyl seat. Tiff pulled her sweat-drenched hair into a ponytail and tried to collect herself while she waited for the driver. Gabriel followed behind her, tracing her steps and pretending to read his play.

A yellow pick-up skidded to a stop next to the Mazda and shook the three from their private dreams. "Good morning, good morning," a lanky man called as he stepped out onto the dirt.

"I thought you would never come," Tiff shouted with a mix of anger and delight. "She's going to bake in there."

"Is this the goat?" The man asked.

"He's doing fine," Tiff replied before stomping back to the car. "Let's get them loaded. They'll call the police if she's not back soon."

Moments later Gabriel was wedged between Stella and the cowboy. In the rearview mirror he watched Tiff settle herself against the Mazda and shrink to nothing.

The third time Gabriel ran away from home he made it all the way to Oregon. His mother had wanted desperately to find him. At the bedside of her waning husband she sat with a pocket full of advertisements for detective agencies she had torn from the phone book. She read them silently to herself by a desk lamp as his eyes fell like tea leaves. In the stillness of that little room her husband asked only that she let him go.

Once in Portland, Gabriel stood underneath a fountain named The Dreamer between Market and Harrison Street. Dozens of boys his age pan-handled with torn backpacks on the curbs as ragged haired girls fished joints out of homemade purses. There had been a pulse; one which had spread across the country pulling children away from Kansas and North Carolina, gathering them West. Gabriel stood among them. Their faces were the same as his. All had come in search of the source of this great feeling. They had followed the spectral pull on their sleeves toward the setting sun and held congress there waiting for the glory of it all. For days they waited for the unknowable to descend, never speaking of it, leaving it unnamed and biding their time sharing beers and stories of their mothers. They had been drawn by an unknowable magnetic wrench which echoed in waves and moved generations in their turn to the end of the continent. And like all other migrations before them, they found it hollow. The promise in their souls remained unfulfilled.

Stella slept for the first time in the truck. Her composure faded as her head slumped against the window. In the privacy of consciousness, the cowboy began to speak.

"So you're the goat?" The cowboy asked.

"I don't know what you're talking about," Gabriel said. "I'm her grandson for the day."

"That's exactly what I'm talking about," The cowboy said. "You ever work on a horse farm?" Gabriel shook his head. "Well if you did you'd know what I mean. You see when you have a real firebrand of a horse, one that bites and kicks, you only have one option. What you have to do is pen them up for awhile until their temper cools. You pen them up in a stall and put a goat in there with them. That little goat keeps them calm. That's what you are."

Tiff's plan began to make more sense. Gabriel had originally agreed to follow them south because it meant a free ride with radicals, which at the time seemed more romantic and exciting than watching other people enjoy their lives by himself. Stella was a fugitive. There would be money for her safe return. He was there to bring her in. He was her grandson. He was her goat.

"When will we bring her back?" Gabriel asked.

"Soon enough," The cowboy said as he pushed his hat back. His knee lifted to the wheel as they swerved into the lines of traffic plunging into massive LA. With one hand he fished a Zippo lighter from his shirt pocket while the other crossed his chest to offer a handshake. "Danny Marcum," he said as Gabriel took his hand. "I'm the best knee driver you'll ever meet."

Stella slept. The bolting of lane changes and brakes jerking did nothing to disrupt her slumber, and her peacefulness appeared so absolute that Gabriel held her out of fear that she would break in her sleep. The palm-lined landscape outside the window was absent of the tourist sites and studio gates he had pictured spanning from the Pacific to the mountains. Danny wheeled his truck off the highway and up hillside roads flanked by abode colored buildings, storage facilities, and desiccated trees.

"She needs her rest," Danny said through the cigarette in his teeth. "It will look better if we bring her in golden and smiling. They'll believe you then."

"Where does she live?" Gabriel said.

"She stays at this retirement village for celebrities. Tiff works there. Top secret place. That's where she got her. If we bring her back before they have to call the police then we've got them."

"I don't understand."

"You will," Danny said as he threw his cigarette out the window.

"Come on now. Let's get a drink." Through the windshield a squat building with bars on the window came into view as the truck came to a stop.

"We can't leave her."

"Hell, man," Danny said as he tipped his cowboy hat down and traced its brim with his fingers in the rearview mirror, "where is she going to go?" Gabriel slid out the driver's side door and followed Danny's strut into the parking lot. "I'll wait here with her. You just go get us a six pack and we'll be on our way." Danny leaned like the rodeo-hand against the truck, and pointed a ten dollar bill at the rusted carry-out sign hanging above the tavern's door.

"I don't have any ID," Gabriel said as he took the money.

"Then take this." Danny reached into his tight jeans and pressed a wedding band into Gabriel's hand. "Tiff said you're down here to act anyway right?"

"What's this for?"

"Just slide that on your ring finger and do like the song says, 'Act Naturally.' That's the best ID a boy can have, goat."

Inside the tavern a few customer in workman clothes hung around corner tables with their heads bowed over long neck bottles. The bartender watched Gabriel move cautiously in from the parking lot, and knew that kids only brought trouble.

"Just a six," Gabriel said. "Don't matter what."

"You're in the wrong place," the bartender said.

Gabriel took the cowboy's advice, and leaned an elbow up on the bar. Then he asked again and slapped the ten dollar bill down flat.

When it looked as if the bartender was about to speak again Gabriel held up his wedding ring.

"Who are you with?" The bartender asked, and eyed the door.

"I'm with a cowboy," Gabriel said. "We're making good time."

The bartender turned to the cooler behind him and slid a six-pack of Tecate over the scratched bar top. "Now you go."

The truck's engine fired up and the three headed back down the blind curves cutting through the hills above freeways that were choked with cars inching along.

"I told you," Danny said. "That was my first fake ID. Works every time."

Gabriel passed Danny a Tecate, and opened one for himself.

"You know for a tramp you have a lot to learn about the world," Danny said as foam spit down his chin. "Yes sir you do."

The morning after his father died, Gabriel awoke in the suit his mother had bought for him in case he ever graduated. The fact that he had left high school his sophomore year for good had done nothing to stop her from believing that someday he would return and pick up the pieces of his young life he had seen fit to scatter to the winds. The suit clung to him after his night's sleep, and as he made his way down to the breakfast table he felt as if all his mother's hopes where stuck to his back.

"He's left us now," Gabriel's mother began. "He's gone." She repeated the fact bluntly to herself while struggling to arrange thank you cards on the table in front of her.

"What are you doing?"

"I have to write thank you notes. There were so many flowers. I have to get them out." Through the kitchen window blackbirds sang to soften their grief. Then, when his mother remembered herself, she looked at him honestly for the first time since he came back. "You've gotten so tall."

Gabriel wanted to apologize. He wanted to explain why he couldn't stand still in one place. He wanted to promise to stay, to go to college, and be a good boy. He wanted to work a summer job and go to church and be normal and plain. He wanted to be all the things his mother had hoped for. But in his chair he could only stare at the dozens of thank you cards waiting to be sent to family members and friends he'd never met. "I am tall."

"Where have you," his mother began then stopped herself. "Did you meet," she began again. It was impossible. She took the first card and began to fill it out slowly in perfect script, then passed it to her son to seal. Together they worked with gratitude for the time they had together.

"Send these away when you have the time," Gabriel's mother said. "They need to be on their way." Later, when Gabriel had left to mail the cards, she broke down. He was gone for good. She could feel it the moment the door closed downstairs.

The truck idled at the gates of the retirement home as Stella woke up. On her face a look of worry settled in and she took Gabriel's hand in hers. Slowly, they walked out to the callbox together.

"Don't forget to be mad as hell," Danny called from the truck. "You have to make them want to settle. They ain't going to want the news to hear about this one you know. They have a reputation to hang on to."

Gabriel clung to Stella's hand and pressed the call button. The gates parted as Danny parked by the curb. "Come on Stella. Let's take you home."

Inside elderly space explorers guided their walkers by action heroes and former center-squares. Grizzled Western stars played checkers with sagging starlets in the dayroom while Stella and Gabriel waited for the director. Orderlies brought them two glasses of orange juice and whispered to one another. By the television a woman stood up and yelled, "It's all fair now!" before being quieted down by the staff.

A handsomely groomed young man in a white suit came to greet them where they sat. "Stella," he said softly, "I'm glad you're home. We all missed you."

"Who are you?" Gabriel asked the man politely.

"I'm the Glamour Soap girl," Stella answered.

"Of course you are," the director said, and then turned to Gabriel.

"I'm her grandson. Just ask her."

"Later," the director said as he helped Stella to her feet. "Now she needs her rest."

Danny had finished the rest of the six-pack in the truck and was jumpy. His hands moved to light another cigarette as he watched Gabriel making his way back down the drive.

"You still want to be a star now?" Danny laughed, but Gabriel didn't answer. "Man! I've heard the stories. So how much did they cut you?"

"What do you mean?" Gabriel said. He got back in the truck, but left his door open. They hadn't closed the gates behind him, and he was glad.

"How much did they write a check for? They have to keep this shit quiet for the insurance and all," Danny said. "They got deep pockets in there. Or did they just slide you some cash?"

"Nothing." Gabriel said. "They said they wouldn't call the police this time was all. They wanted to know who took her. She's got health problems you know."

"Nothing? What do you mean nothing?"

"You got a lot to learn," Gabriel said as he tossed the wedding ring onto the dashboard.

"Well fuck Tiff, and fuck you too!" Danny yelled before looking around as if the boy wee part of one big set-up. "What's my name?"

"I don't know what you mean."

"What did I tell you my name was?"

"I don't remember," Gabriel said. "You're just some dumb cowboy."

"That's the right answer," Danny said. "Just some dumb cowboy."

Gabriel picked up his book and got out of the truck. He started back toward the gate before Danny hollered for him to come back.

"So what now?" Danny asked as Gabriel stood outside his window. "What do I do with a goat like you after the horse has run off?"

Gabriel pulled a cigarette out of Danny's pocket, and stuck his head in for a light. Danny obliged. "Now you ride off into the sunset," Gabriel said as he worked out his character in his head. "She needs someone to stay with her."

"They won't let you back in there. Don't be ignorant. They'll have someone come and pick you up if you go back in there."

"She needs to be with her family until she finds her way back." Gabriel tossed his cigarette to the ground and started back toward the gate.

"You go in there and it's a one way ticket to county," Danny said. "That's your charge. Keep my name out of your mouth, and Tiff's too."

"I can forget anyone," Gabriel said, and put up a hand as Danny spun off.

When the receptionist saw Gabriel come back inside she turned her head and picked up the phone. The orderlies who had brought him orange juice earlier casually walked to block the door. Stella was still in the dayroom. When she saw him she glowed, and took his hands into hers. An elderly man began to play the piano, and on cue she sang to him with a voice full and untouched by time. The other residents heard her song, and were drawn to her. Every man and woman who could make it to the day room in the home for wayward celebrities joined together and sang. Their voices floated through the ceiling above, and carried them into the past.

About the Author

Michael Wayne Hampton is the author of three books. His criticism, essays, fiction, and poetry have appeared in numerous publications such as *Atticus Review, The Southeast Review, 3AM Magazine,* and *Fiction Southeast.* In 2013 he won The Deerbird Novella Prize, and in 2012 his work was nominated for *Best American Short Stories.* In the past he has been a semi-finalist for the Iowa Short Fiction Prize, and a two-time Finalist for the World's Best Short Short Story Contest. He grew up in the hills of eastern Kentucky, and received his BA in English from the University of Kentucky before earning his MFA in Writing from Spalding University. He currently serves as an Assistant Professor of English at the University of Cincinnati Clermont College where he has won, or been nominated for, several teaching and service awards.